MW00883923

'TIS MORE THAN LUCK

A NOVEL

BY
J. E. DELEHANTY

This novel is a work of fiction. Any names, characters, places, and incidents are the product of this author's imagination and are used fictitiously. Any resemblance to real events, locations, or persons either living or dead is purely coincidental

Printed by CreateSpace

Copyright © 2016 by John E Delehanty

All rights are reserved. No part of this publication may be reproduced, stored, or transmitted in any form or by any means without prior written permission of the author

ISBN - 13:9781533036278

Questions and/or comments may be directed to the author at mrgus0150@gmail.com

The cover design is an original work of art by Frankie White and may not be reproduced in any form without the express permission of the artist herself

Jack is originally from Minnesota but moved to the Northwest with his family when he was young. He completed his undergraduate work at Gonzaga University with a double major in English and Theater, received his MA in Theater Arts from Washington State University and continued his doctoral studies at Northwestern University. An educator for over thirty years, Jack devoted his life to teaching English and Theater to young people. He is an actor, director and devoted supporter of theater on all levels.

This is Jack's first novel. It is the culmination of 20 years of work and although the novel is completely fictitious, it reflects his own roots, his love of family and the gifts they have given him and the beauty of the Irish soul. It is his sincere hope that you love his story as much as he has loved creating it.

FOREWARD

The Spirit Within

Much of the ancient celtic beliefs still characterize the Irish soul including the belief that every single thing be it person or place, living or non-living, has a spirit within that not only influences but actually enters our lives. So it is for our young Jack. The spirit within the people who populate his small world whether they are young or old; the places that are his geography whether familiar or new; the things that surround him whether tractor or town or funeral or flute not only influence his life but alter its course and determine who he becomes. As it might be said of all our lives, "'Tis more than luck surely."

PROLOGUE

*The longest road out is
the shortest road home*

I was in no hurry. I had waited a long time to return. I looked much like what you would expect to find in a middle-aged farm boy of Irish descent. The years of city living and teaching in a private school had not erased the shape of the small town youth. I was prepared to be sentimental and in fact, like a good little Irishman, I had spent all morning working myself into a fine melancholy mood just for the occasion. The plan was that I would take a long walk down memory lane. I was prepared to conjure it all up and to shake hands with both the good and the bad.   I was intending to have my heart strings tugged, dance on a few graves, and even cry for more than a few lost loves. All together it promised to be a day I had been putting off for too many years and one that, for my own sense of self, could be delayed no longer.

I came up the old driveway that led to the top of the hill. I might have missed the road altogether if not for the mailbox slanted out of a rusted milk can. The bottom of the box had given way but it still stood ready, impaled on the rotting post. The letters J period LA were still visible beneath years of neglect. The once red-tipped flag was up as though someone were still expecting the postman to stop. I'd go on foot from here. I would rake my feet across the soil that had soaked up the blood and sweat of my family and that had ground itself into the creases of my youth. I would run my hands across the old boards that had absorbed the rain and wind of the unforgiving years and the memories of a young boy who had left them behind.

I leaned against the mail box looking like I waited here everyday for news from the past. The hog farm across the road looked prosperous and much as I remembered it. What lay up the hill at my back, I knew, would be a different story. "Old MacLaney had a farm e-i-e-i…" I shaded my eyes and looked up to the long white streamers high in the morning sky and watched as a hawk circled familiar hunting ground. He would have a better view than I, I thought, but I would be able to walk the old path down to the well and follow the creek to the edge of Lake Cullen, named after a larger and more beautiful lake in Ireland, and step on the boards of the porch that afforded a view of the meadows and the hills that rolled into the searing sky.

As I turned to start up the hill and see what could be found of a time gone by, a giant pawed black lab puppy raced out of the weeds and ran in circles around me. Since he was still with me half way up the hill, I decided the two of us could make this trip together. In fact, the over excited lab nipping at my heals might just be the perfect combination.

"Come on then, pup, you stick with me and I'll tell you what it was like when I was as young and excited as you are. We'll walk the fields and kick, or sniff, at the neglected relics of a different time, a long ago time, a time of great miserable joy."

I had planned on meeting only one person on this journey and that one would not arrive for several hours yet. How was I to guess there were to be many more who would appear? Discovered in straight backed chairs long since gone listening to a phantom radio. Heard from the dusty shadows of crumbling sheds and caved-in wells and broken reminders of roots tapped deep. They would come. They would come, so real I would smell their tears and hear their happy sorrow.

CHAPTER 1

There is no need to fear the wind
if your haystacks are tied down

When I was a boy, I knew from long practice that the only way to deal with the morning chill was to slide my arm out from under the quilt and retrieve the overalls and flannel shirt from the floor where I had dropped them the night before. Once I accomplished this, being careful to expose only one arm, I pulled the damp clothes under the covers and, using the big toe of my left foot, pushed them to the end of the bed and left them to warm while I lay still and listened to the sounds of the farm and its two-story house waking up.

~ ~ ~ ~

I was still too young to have gathered any cynicism about the reality of where I lived or about the people who textured my life. The stale odor of urine from chamber pots too infrequently emptied and soiled clothes less frequently washed permeated the damp walls that could no longer hold the faded and flowered paper.   The close, musty air fought against the smell of wood smoke that had seeped from the old Monarch stove for sixty years.   On Monday the stench of lye rose up and took control of the house, the clothes, and the yard.   If the wind were coming from behind the outhouse, it was impossible to smell even the odor of the chicken coop.   The smells seemed to mix and mingle so that the trail of my Uncle Shay's (I never heard him called Seamus) stale tobacco juice in the parlor spittoon was indistinguishable from the malignant odor of sickness that drifted from the room where my three great aunts lay dying.

The farm had been on a slow but constant march toward death for fifteen years and none of the ten or so people who might have turned it around seemed to care.   It was noticeable, of course, only in the little things that hid behind the scenes.   The relatives who drove down from the Twin Cities on weekend visits never noticed the corncrib door that creaked lazily back and forth on one hinge like an idle schoolboy on the bus stop post.   Nor did they pay attention to the chickens that now pecked loose in the yard instead of within the wire mesh fence Aunt Jane had been so proud of when she was well.   They didn't hear the tin roof on the slightly listing barn clang and bang with a distant lonesome sound.   The fact that the well was still at the bottom of the hill below the barnyard seemed to concern no one and they never bothered to comment that in 1955 there was still no running water, no indoor plumbing and a crank telephone that should have been in a local antique shop.

Judge J. Thomas Laney's farm had once been a

showplace of Beaumont County. The two-story frame house had sat, white and clean, on top of the hill in front of the gleaming red and white outbuildings. The manicured green lawn had run all the way down to the road. On warm Saturday nights, the polished buggies of the county's most important people would circle through that lawn and come to stop in front of the long veranda. Only the finest cigars were smoked on those summer evenings, their pungent sweetness drifting with the political and agricultural talk catching the quiet feminine laughter floating out of the front parlor and, mingling, they would settle over the corn and alfalfa in a comfortable way, for they were all rooted together in the soil of that Irish farming community.

Those days had passed now, alive only in the memories of my great aunts who would die believing the whitewashed fence still ran the length of the front slope and that the house still stood as it had, a white and stately symbol of prestige and authority.

~ ~ ~ ~

I knew nothing of what I know now as I lay snug in the depth of my patchwork quilt. The nostrils of my youth were not assailed by smells of decay and neglect.   They were, instead, filled with the wonderfully comfortable aromas of the people and pleasures that made my life whole.   When we are young we listen, we touch, we sniff, we watch, and we grow hungry. For many it is the clamorous excitement that rushes through city streets and crowded urban dwellings.   For some it is the easy, rambling of the small town strutting itself and relaxing back to a sleepy gait. My world was the slow throb of a constant heartbeat~even, routine, and flooded with life. The sights, sounds, and smells changed throughout the day, repeated themselves the next with always the same rhythm. It was a rhythm I depended on, waited for, took comfort in. I knew those rhythms. I remember them as though my head were still resting on that down pillow. The mornings were always special. I waited now in my bed for the rhythm to begin.

The commanding bark of Lewis, my fat black lab, herding Aunt Jane's Road Island Reds into a state of panic and confusion. The clang of cast iron skillets soon to be heated by the newly stoked applewood laid in the stove. The bang of the back screen door and the shuffle scrape of Uncle Shay's shoes on the cinder walk. I could visualize my aproned Aunt Mary, her steps choreographed over the years, moving across the well-worn paths of her kitchen. She was a comfortable woman to watch. A large woman at close to six feet tall, she did not move quickly or lightly but, rather, like Lark the old work horse, gently slow and beautiful in her controlled and purposeful movements. Like Lark, too, there was a dignity in the way she began each morning and ended each day, taking what pride she could from tedious and thankless work. Had my Aunt Mary lived in a later time, she might well have strutted her six foot frame down Washington Mall, banner in hand and my Uncle Shay may have considered, if not washing, at least folding his own socks. But she was a victim of her own time and place, her growth both nurtured and stunted by her chance placement in the world.

My aunt's face may have told me some of this had I been able to see the depth of sadness in her eyes or hear it in the tones of her voice. But I saw none of it.   I heard none of it.   Perhaps, in her wisdom, she allowed only the walls of her spotless kitchen and the night darkness of her bedroom to read such things in her weathered countenance. What I did see were strong, capable hands marked even then with rough callouses and ridges.   They had grown coarse as much from scrubbing with strong, granulated soap as from work. To me, she smelled of flour, wood smoke, and love.   She might have been beautiful or she may never have been anything but plain.   The images that passed through my mind as I did my slow wakeup routine above her had nothing to do with that kind of physical attribute and, as far as I know, her youthful visage was framed only in the memory of my Uncle Shay who courted young Mary Shields in the wake of new mown hay. Now she was simply Aunt Mary and she called upstairs in her deep rasping voice. "Jackie, chores awaitin'."

I pulled on my now warm clothes, danced across the cold linoleum to the chamber pot and slid down the banister into the world that had a strange and wonderful impact on my life. I pumped ice cold water into the bowl and pretended to splash some of it on my face. "Morning, Aunt Mary." I started to towel my still dry face to make it look good.

"Use the soap and scrub some color into those cheeks, Jackie."   Without looking toward me she pushed the cinnamon rolls into the oven. It was an innocent move but I knew what she was saying clear enough. If I didn't wash up for real, the rolls would be withheld. I splashed the cold water on my face and scrubbed with diligence. Anyone with any sense at all would swim an ice cold river for those rolls or for anything else she cooked.

By the time I had returned from the well, balancing two buckets of splashing water, my mother and father had filled their cups with hot tea and were spooning in the fresh cream. I had learned early that carrying two buckets was easier than carrying one. As I came up the hill one morning, listing badly to one side, my single bucket already half empty from splashing over, my grandfather stepped out of the milk shed and stopped me.

"Johnny, you'll do much better if you carry two buckets instead of one," he said.

~ ~ ~ ~

For some reason, which I have yet to understand, I was Jackie to all the women in my early life and Johnny to all the men. My mother reserved John Edward for very special occasions. Whenever she used that name I knew that whatever I was doing had better stop or whatever I wasn't doing had better start. Stranger still was the habit all the adults in my life had, with the exception of my mother and father, of referring to me as "The Boy." My aunt would say, "The Boy needs to finish his breakfast." My uncle: "The Boy won't stop yammerin' about that damn tractor." My grandfather was always saying, "The Boy's got to learn." I thought nothing of it and actually often thought of myself as The Boy.

~ ~ ~ ~

"Two buckets, Grandpa?" I said. "I can't hardly get up the hill with one."

"Two, Johnny. It's much easier." He turned back to the shed. It didn't take long to find out that he was right. He was always right. That was the thing about grandfathers, they were always right, it seemed, and they made so little show of it.

There was no need to call everyone to the breakfast table. We all seemed to have some kind of inner clock that had been synchronized at birth with meal times. I don't remember anyone ever being late to my Aunt Mary's table. We came like leghorns, scurrying through the hall door, out of the living room, in from the yard, and pecked around without purpose until the silent alarm went off and we all bobbled to the table. Aunt Mary had eaten first and had taken the trays into the "Aunties". Using the ends of her apron as hot pads, she hustled the hot serving plates to us and just as quickly we emptied them onto our own plates.

Like all farm families, we had only two big meals each day, breakfast and dinner. Supper was usually a cold meal and much lighter than the other two. Breakfast and dinner were important socially as well as nutritionally. As I watched the butter flow in between the swirls of my cinnamon roll and licked at the white glaze, I was unaware of how important those meals were.

The conversation was subdued during the first moments of concentrated eating, but soon settled into the clamor of thirteen people all trying to be heard.

My grandfather generally served as moderator, drawing the conversation this way or that. I can look through the family album now and see what he looked like. A fringe of close cropped white hair around a smooth head. Looking at the picture now, I see my father in his later years. Cutting off the forehead and chin, I find the resemblance remarkable. The wide narrow mouth, the lower lip protruding slightly, the nose, the eyes all the same. They are expressive eyes, eyes that dance with mischievous delight and shimmer with a hidden Irish temper. But most of all, eyes that continually reflect a depth of gentleness and compassion that lay at the root of my grandfather and that continued to grow in my father. The album picture shows only a part of both men, however. There is another picture that remains equally as truthful and equally as erroneous as the snapshot. Time has yellowed and faded the picture in the album. The image that was formed in my youth, however, is clear. Yet, neither of these portraits is quite the truth. I know much of my grandfather that I did not know at thirteen. I know now of his human weaknesses, of his stubbornness, and of his unconscious cruelty. I know now of my father's narrow escape from beneath the weight of his father's dominant personality. Time erodes the photo paper and clouds the truth and memory is a selective process, but my youthful images seem to me to be the most dependable.

As I sat across the table and listened to him orally rebuild the barn and its surrounding buildings, I caught the wink he gave me and I knew we would hunt together on Sunday. He would wear, as would my father, heavy canvas pants, their weight held up by old button suspenders above a worn out dress shirt. His baldness would be protected by a gray, rumpled fedora, brim bent down in the front not so much from the style as from the constant putting on and taking off and the force of bad weather.   Crooked under his right arm would be 'old madam', the model ninety-seven Winchester with the hair trigger. We would take lunch, extra shells, and our time. Even today, walking beside my father on city streets, stretching to keep up with his long stride, I am reminded of my grandfather. I remember, too, later times, times beyond my grandfather, when my own father and I would hunt for birds together. I would watch him moving through the brush off to the side of me, so much like his father. The hunting times were good times.

My stomach clutched with anticipation, but that would be Sunday and today had a specialness all its own,   I seldom spent much time anticipating the future because each day was full. I used to think that I was a great help to everyone on the farm and counted my chores as crucial to the overall operation. Looking back, I realize I was in the way more than anything else.   Somehow, however, across the cornfields, meadows, and woods of those one hundred and sixty acres, I found enough adventures, mysterious places, and fulfilled dreams to make all of my early days complete. I had no suspicion, those first days of summer, that winds were already gathering and were about to blow across my gentle fields and change the landscape of my life forever.

CHAPTER II

You'll never plow a field by turning
it over in your mind

A deliberate turn of his head to the left allowed just the split second of time needed to judge distance, velocity, and direction. The brownish blob of tobacco juice hit nine inches from his left foot and rolled mercurially in the dirt like a small oil slick before it was sweetly sucked home by the parched Minnesota earth. I kept my head down, watching that spreading stain, and waited. Anticipation tugged at every nerve end in my body.

With a practiced toe of his worn black work shoe, my Uncle Shay flicked the dirt to cover his mark and tried my patience by slowly repeating the entire process twice more. The morning was still cool, but beneath the metal roof of the tractor shed, the temperature was rising quickly. As the second red brown stain slowly disappeared, a few drops of sweat fell from my forehead and formed little craters in the dust at my feet.   This was no time to betray my feelings.   If anything happened to change the course of planned events this morning, I would likely die. This was the promised day, the appointed hour, the very moment of my greatest joy and greatest fear. To my right, my future awaited me.   To my left, the baggy overalled, bristled old man who could lead me to it. This complex man caught in a world of farming and the repetitive tedium it demanded was finding a simple joy in toying with his desperate nephew.   He had never seen a play and, probably, few films.   Yet, he had, innately, a fine sense of the dramatic.   It has been said that what life ultimately lacks is a well placed climax.   Not so with my Uncle Shay around. Somehow, in the plowing of his fields and the pulling of his milk cow's teats, he had come to understand the subtle and selective elements of dramatic timing. When he was in his playwright mode, as he was this morning, he could structure a script and its performance with the best of them.   He had already done the opening very well.   Working his wad of tobacco and the calculated ejections that followed had dimmed the houselights, opened the curtain, and played the first measures of the overture all at the same time.   Soon, now, he would move into careful exposition and the first elements of tension and conflict.

I waited while he moseyed over a few steps and placed a worn gloved hand on the tractor. He rubbed gently with his fingertips as if idly scratching behind a pet's ear, spit once more for effect, then stared at me until I looked up.

"Now, ya' see this flywheel here?" He questioned very seriously. "I venture to say it weighs half again what you do, Johnny."

He moved along past the step up and stood facing me.

"And this lug wheel, here, is a good head taller than your puny frame. The lugs are ten in all on each side, each one as big as my fist. Its six feet and one half inches up to the seat and the whole tractor is as long as a team of Morgans, traces and all."

Here he gathered his cheeks together and planted a stream right in front of my feet.

"You want to climb up then, Johnny?"

This was it. I was not a rational thirteen year old. I was all emotions and anticipation come to the boil. I turned my eyes like street lamps toward my uncle and started for the tractor. To put things in perspective, this was not simply a tractor. It was the first bike for a city kid, the first car for a teenager, the first girlfriend for any boy, and the sun and the moon and the stars for me. This was the John Deere, the "Johnny Popper," and, if all went well, this was the day I would drive it by myself.

But he put his hand out before I could get a step up and pushed in front of me. "Now, before we get hasty," he said, "there are a few things you ought to know about the 'Johnny Popper'."

"Ah, Uncle Shay, I've watched you for weeks now and I know how ta do it. I've watched real careful, Uncle Shay."

He considered this as he worked the tobacco in his cheek then he nodded. "Ya have, have ya?"

If I had been a dog like my black lab, Lewis, my tail would have been high and happy and my tongue would have been working up a real lather. As it was, I couldn't contain myself much longer and all the pretense of nonchalance had given way to pure desire. I was about to burst and he knew it.

"Well, let's get to it before ya wet yer pants."

I went past him not knowing where my feet lit and found myself sitting high above the ground, the huge black steering wheel locked in my grip. She was so big and beautiful. I bounced up and down on the spring seat and laughed right out loud. I worked the throttle and stretched my legs to reach the pedals, pushing in and out hardly noticing the effort it took. Finally, I settled enough to look down at my uncle who was studying me with as much expression as his taciturn nature allowed.

"Do I have all day, Uncle Shay? All morning? Can we hook up the plow or the rake?"

"Oh, you could have all mornin' I 'spect. We better wait on hookin' anything on at the start though." He stopped and just kept looking at me like he expected me to say something.

"You do have one small problem though, Johnny," he said. I wasn't dismayed. I knew there was no problem I couldn't overcome. Nothing would keep me from my appointed destiny. I was to be the tractor driver of all time. The best in the family. The best in Beaumont County. Perhaps the best in the whole state. So it was with great confidence I asked, "What problem, Uncle Shay?"

As he stepped over to the huge tool box that was

fastened to the side of the tractor, he said, "This is a workin' machine, Johnny. She's 160 horsepower and all muscle. She'll plow all day and all night and do it day in and day out for just about as long as you can imagine."

He took a long bent bar out of the box and let the lid fall shut.

"She won't do that for ya, however, unless ya start her up first. It's a funny thing, Johnny, but unless she's runnin', nothin' happens. That's it. She just sits there and nothin' happens."

Undaunted, I said, "O.K., let's start her up."

"Yup, she'll sure do a day's work all right. No feedin' this one or restin' her in the heat of the day. All work, that's what she's all about. But, then, there are a few ifs that are involved, Johnny."

"Ifs?" I said.

He nodded as he handed me the metal crank. "Uh, huh. If ya can turn this flywheel over and if ya can turn it enough times and if ya can turn it fast enough. If ya can do all that, chances are she'll start and then yer on yer way. And then, of course, if ya can't do all that...."

He just left the rest hanging. I might have simply asked him if he would turn it for me or if maybe my cousin Will could do it if he weren't out in the fields yet, or maybe even Dad, if he were around. But I knew better. My heart sank and my excitement disappeared in the sunbaked heat of the shed. I knew my Uncle Shay. I also knew the farm and something of how a person took his place in its straight-forward approach to life. There was no vocabulary like "macho" or "passages" or "maturation," just a simple, built-in framework that was followed by all boys who expected to become men and all girls who wanted to be women. You couldn't break out of it, not even if a man such as Uncle Shay had cared to help you. It was crystal clear to me that I was going to have to start the tractor if I ever wanted to drive it. It was equally clear that my chances of doing it were slim.

I looked at the crank in my small hands and worked my throat and facial muscles every way possible trying to hold back the tears of defeat and disappointment . It was shaping up to be that kind of summer for me.   All kinds of events and people pushing me this way and that and all I wanted to do was drive that tractor. It had nothing to do with being a man that I could see. I just wanted it, that's all. All that power and it turning this way or that just when you wanted it to. And the places you could go....

"Damn," I said.

"Here now, boy, your aunt's just around the corner with the hens and we'll have none of that kind of language."

Nobody on the farm was particularly profane, especially my uncle. It was all right to cuss a bit in the fields or in town or in the outhouse, but not so much and never around the women. The soap was always handy and the women ready to use it.

I jumped off the seat and threw the crank against the back wall as I turned to run full tilt to my favorite sulking place. Pigs are not particularly compassionate or feeling animals, but nobody seemed to go around the pens much, so I could be alone there. Besides, it was in full view of the yard and the house and everyone could see me there and feel great pity for whatever injustice had been laid upon me. It often worked, especially with my dad. But, I wasn't after any attention this time, I just naturally ran to the pigs in time of personal sorrow.

I don't know how long I sulked there before I heard the fence board creak next to me and saw the tobacco juice hit the side of an old sow.

"Ya know, if ya let that lower lip drag in this slop, ya could get a mean infection, Johnny."

"I just wanna drive it, Uncle Shay, and she's gotta be taken out anyway. Why couldn't someone just start it up for me?"

He didn't say anything for a long time and I was thinking up other pleas when he took out his soiled hanky and handed it to me.

"I was sixteen when I realized I wanted to be a major league ballplayer. Did ya know I almost played major league, Johnny?" He didn't wait for my answer. "Well, I wanted to in the worst way. I knew I was good. I'd had a good coach and my brother, your granddad, and I were about the best in the state. Well, a scout came through one season and watched me play in the state finals over in Faribault. He came at the right time, too, because I played good, real good."

Stories were a great part of my Uncle Shay. Most of the tales I had heard a few times over, but this one was new. He had a way about him, a sincerity that always captivated me. I had stopped thinking about the tractor. It was just Uncle Shay and another good story and me leaning on the pigpen.

"Well," he went on, "this scout came up to talk to me after that game.   He was a redheaded fella wearing one of those seersucker suits and a smile as big as an acre. The upshot was that he reckoned that I was material for the majors."

Here he paused and aiming at the nearest pig, he spat again. "Inside, of course, I couldn't have agreed more and I knew I was going to accept whatever offer he had." There was another long pause and another spit.

"Problem was, he didn't offer me a ticket to Brooklyn. What he said was, he thought I ought to go up to this farm team in St. Paul and kinda get my feet wet, prove myself, he said. Well, I wanted to play for the majors, Johnny, with all the life that was in me. I was ready to give up my girlfriend, my family, everything just to have a chance in the majors."

There was a long pause. Then, after a time, I looked up at him as he put his foot down and turned to go.

"Hey, Uncle Shay," I said, wanting an end to the story. "Did you get to the majors then?"

He stopped but didn't turn around.   "Nope.   I never did, Johnny."

I jumped off the fence and ran around to grab his sleeve and get a look at his face. "Jeeze, why not?" I asked.

But he moved on past me and threw over his shoulder, so that I barely caught it, "I was afraid, Johnny, afraid to turn the crank."

CHAPTER III

*Neither give cherries to pigs
nor advice to a fool*

"Working the dogs," he called it. It was not hunting season, but always in my grandfather's mind, hunting season was only a few days away. He carried a Winchester model 97, my father carried a Remington model 12, and I carried a single shot 20 gauge of unknown origin.

"If you can't get what you're after in one shot, Johnny," my grandfather would say, "you've got no business being out here."

I had never questioned this. As a matter of fact, I never questioned my grandfather at all. I did wonder vaguely why I was the only one with a single shot gun, but it was only a passing thought. The truth is I always took whatever my father or my grandfather offered at face value. My father moved somewhat in the shadow of my grandfather. At the time, I didn't see it so much as fear on his part as unwavering respect. Since I sensed it as such, I tried to give the same to my father in turn. We made a very compatible trio. Respect, after all, was the nature of the game. Respect for the dogs, respect for nature, respect for firearms, respect for your fellow hunters. We made a very respectful team.

The guns were not loaded, of course. It was all show for the dogs. We would not see the golden bloom of Autumn for several months. We would not feel the edge of Winter in the morning air or turn our collars up in afternoons that came more quickly to an end. It was not time to hunt together yet. Still, I was happy to pre-empt that season for whatever reason. I was happy to spend my time beside these two men no matter what the occasion.

~ ~ ~ ~

I watched my father now as we moved across the lower pasture and headed toward the woods. It was difficult to imagine the farm without these two men and harder still to imagine a world without the farm. To the passerby, she was only a quarter section of land a short distance from the typical farming town of Kilkerry in Southwestern Minnesota, dotted with a few buildings and peopled by those who received their Montgomery Ward's catalogue in the ubiquitous mailbox stuck in an old milk can at the end of the drive. To the eye of the red-tailed hawk who soared the currents of the warm evening's air, she was a bountiful patchwork of corn and grain and pasture, the square section lines broken only by the gentle sweep of Cow Creek as it snaked its way to the marsh at the edge of a lake too small to be counted in the ten thousand. A few of the old gentlemen who gathered in the afternoon on the porch of the old hotel in town might remember her by the smell of plum and apple and lilac that would have greeted her early visitors as they came up the drive to the two-story frame house that sat perched atop a knoll, its railed porches like the bridge of an old square rigger.

She was not quite torn from the pages of a coffee table book on Ireland. But, like a fisherman's sweater, she was knitted by the calloused hands of simple people. They wore her because she was familiar. They loved her and needed her, hated her for her coarseness, found comfort in her well-worn security. She smelled of the earth and the animals that made up her threads and the sweat produced by her weight. She was well used but fashioned to endure.

We were part of her, my father, my grandfather, and I, woven into her, inexorably a part of her. I felt it on that day as we crossed the ditch at the end of the field and spread out to enter the woods. Comfortable. A sense of belonging that warmed my blood and tickled my stomach. My father would take the right side, my grandfather the left, and I would take the middle. I don't recall when it had been established that way. It simply was the way it was and no one had to speak of it. Both my father and my grandfather were wearing their field jackets and canvas pants in spite of the heat.

~ ~ ~ ~

"To please the dogs," they said.

My father carried his gun crooked across his right arm, his long strides covering ground at a pace he could maintain all day without tiring. My grandfather's was crooked in the opposite direction and I carried mine resting over my arm and pointed at the ground. The dogs worked their familiar patterns, muzzles to the ground, tongues dripping, tails collecting twigs and burrs and snarls. Pat, the Irish Setter, worked out in front of the two labs. She was the only one who went on point and could actually hold the birds. The other two had to be constantly held back to keep them from flushing the birds too soon. They had all been hunting for a long time and knew what was expected of them. But on this first "practice" morning they were all overanxious. My lab, Lewis, was the least disciplined of them all. He thrashed through the underbrush fifty yards ahead of us, either driving the birds out in front of him before Pat could hold them or flushing them up so far ahead of us that a clear shot would have been impossible.

"Call Lewis back," my father yelled, "he's out too far."

Calling Lewis back would be as easy as changing the law of gravity and we all knew that, but it was part of the ritual that got us ready for the fall and the real events that would then take place. My grandfather was less kind.

"Damn mutt! I'd shoot him now if my gun were loaded."

He didn't mean it, I knew. He liked to grumble and bluster. He saw it not only as his right, but as his responsibility. Everyone was in high spirits. When the young birds exploded from the underbrush, a thunder of flapping wings, we all reacted according to our training and instincts. The dogs froze waiting for the shots. The guns came up and out, then were thrown back into the shoulder to follow the flight of the gliding bird. We made little boom, boom sounds to imitate the sound of the firing guns and let out our breath knowing we had bagged another three birds. The Minnesota farmland of my youth was rich, not only in the harvest of crops, but in game as well. I had never accompanied my cousin when he tagged his annual deer, but I loved hunting pheasant and duck. To me, the birds were beautiful, the skill a challenge, and the downing of a bird in flight an exhilarating experience. I had not yet been touched by a guilty sense of "killing for sport." I went at it with the same red-eyed heat that surely coursed through the veins of the mammoth hunters, mad for a moment, I suppose, and thrilled by that link with my baser instincts. On those practice days, though, there was no killing, just the warmth of sun and companionship, Lewis panting around me in joyous circles, and a taste of what Fall would bring.

We came to the edge of the woods where it gave way to pasture that had been cleared as far as Lake Cullen. The wooded acres ended on a slight rise so that the pasture sloped gently to the shore of the small lake. There were stumps and fallen logs near the trees. Always the perfect place for our lunch stop, a stop that extended into time for a bowl of tobacco and serious "man talk," that time so belittled by contemporary psychologists and labelled as "male bonding." Whatever the psychological ramifications, it was always a pleasant time for me. I usually heard little of the conversation carried on by the two older men. I would stroke the sleek back of Lewis and gaze off across the lake, daydreaming about anything that made me feel good inside. Sometimes it was about the farm, sometimes about the mysterious things Fr. Shea would tell about in his lilting voice, and, lately, about my cousin Essie or Morgan Phiffer. I threw sticks for the dogs to retrieve because they never tired of the game for which they were bred. I slept, I dreamed, I soaked up whatever came my way.

"We'll have to shoot The Boy's dog before Fall comes," my grandfather said with a broad wink to my father.

"Either that or tie him up before we go out, I guess," said my father as he continued to tease me.

"He's got a softer mouth than any of the others," which is what I always said in Lewis's defense. "And besides, you don't shoot something you love, Grandpa."

"Umm. I suppose you're right, Johnny. Well, maybe we'll just have to leave him home from now on."

I looked at my father to make sure the game was still being played and was glad to see him smile as he knocked the bowl of his pipe on the heel of his boot. My grandfather stood and scratched behind the ears of the dogs who nudged at his legs, eager to be at it again.

"Well, any birds that Lewis pushed out in front of us should be in that hedgerow along to the right. Let the dogs work the middle. Johnny, you and your dad take the right, I'll go up the left. Hold Lewis in now, this will be our last chance before we reach the lake."

The dogs started out just like they knew what Grandpa had said, Pat crisscrossed out ahead of the other two, glimpses of her red-gold tail flashing in the sun like real Autumn color. Dad moved a few yards out into the pasture and I hugged the edge of the brush. I could vaguely hear Grandpa grumbling to himself off to the right and calling to the labs, holding them back 'til Pat went on point. The roar of the pheasant's wings was familiar to all of us, but there was always that startled flinch and wild jump in my stomach even after hundreds of times. The rush of adrenaline and then the instincts took over. We had covered almost all the ground before reaching the shore when I saw the setter go on point.

~ ~ ~ ~

All field dogs are beautiful to watch. The centuries of breeding culminate each time in an exquisite portrait of precision and style. The setter has a point all its own. Not as rigid as the pointers, but the control is every bit as magnificent. The muzzle drawn outward toward the scent, the hind legs back thrusting the whole body toward the mark, willing that small prey into stillness, commanding it. The right paw lifted and bent back, the first move of the flush already completed.

~ ~ ~ ~

We kept moving, holding the labs back, ready in case the birds would not hold. Then my father waved his hand and all three dogs broke to flush the birds. I saw the flash of color before I heard the sound. My gun was off my shoulder, my finger releasing the safety as I pulled the stock back into my shoulder. For the first time that day, perhaps to test myself, perhaps from force of habit, I pulled the hammer of the single shot gun back as I sighted the bird and began to squeeze the trigger. When the bird was covered I tightened the squeeze.

I saw clearly in what my grandfather called, "the eye of the shooter," that it was not a pheasant. I recognized the long neck, the sweep of the wings, and the iridescent green marking of the wood duck. Just as my father yelled, "duck!," the stock recoiled into my shoulder and the sound of my shot, the real sound, boomed out over the lake in a loud echo then died on the far shore as the drake folded his wings and dropped into the reeds at the edge of the lake.

From a great distance, as though I were standing and watching and listening through a thick mist, I heard the dogs barking, my grandfather thrashing his way through the thicket and my father's voice as he ran toward me.

"Hell on a damn crutch," he cursed. "What in the Sam Hell...Dad over here, watch the ditch....Johnny? Johnny? Damn...!"

I don't remember anyone touching me or shaking me, just voices from a long way off for what seemed like a long time, hours perhaps or days. Then the mist cleared and I was looking into the flashing eyes of Lewis standing in front of me. He barked twice then muzzled something on the ground at my feet, pushing it toward me as if to say, "Here, take it. It's yours."

I looked at the once beautiful bird dropped at my feet. The neck was twisted over its back, its feathers ripped and frayed by buckshot and covered with mud and saliva from the dog's mouth. Lewis waited for his accolade, some indication from me that he had done well. Instead I kicked at the bloodied carcass and kicked again and again at the dirt trying to cover it up as I screamed, "It's ugly! They're ugly! They're all ugly!"

My father pulled me back and reached to pick up my gun.

"I'll get the bird and the gun, Jim. You take The Boy up in the shade where he can sit for a bit. Go on," he encouraged, "I'll take care of this."

We all just sat there. The three of us stared at the ground like we were in the dentist's office or something. The flies buzzed around the back of Grandpa's field jacket and a few cows moved across the pasture toward the water. Nobody said anything for a long time. I had been fighting to keep my churning stomach in its place, the bile burning my throat as I swallowed it down. Finally, Dad handed me the burlap covered water bottle and after we had all had a drink, we got up and headed toward the house. I followed behind a few paces, vaguely aware of the subdued conversation in front of me. I was empty handed. My grandfather carried both his gun and mine. I didn't care. I didn't want to see that gun ever again. Not for a million years. Yet, it seemed unfair to take my gun, I didn't know it was loaded.

"I checked it, Grandpa. Honest. I checked it twice."

My grandfather looked back and nodded. My father dropped back and put his arm around my shoulder, but nobody said anything. Well, what could they have said? I had shot a duck out of season. I had shot a bird protected by the State of Minnesota. There would be a huge fine, perhaps I'd go to prison. And, worst of all, I was carrying a loaded gun that was supposed to be empty. I saw myself in front of the Game Warden, describing how I had gone to the gun cabinet that morning, broken my gun open and pointed it toward the window to look down the barrel. He shook his head from side to side in silent disbelief. I looked toward the two men who would defend me but their backs were turned. I went to my knees and explained that I always cleaned my gun before we went out for the day. I had cleaned it that morning, I said, tears running down my face. And, still, he shook his head from side to side and, still, the backs that might have turned to save me did not. The warden's huge hand grabbed the shirt behind my neck and began to drag me from the room as I yelled, "It wasn't loaded! It wasn't loaded!"

"It happens, Johnny," my father crooned as he rocked me in his arms. "No matter how careful we think we are, it happens. We'll sort it all out, son. We'll figure it all out later."

My grandfather hurrumphed as he ruffled my hair. "Reminds me, I gotta fix that damn hair trigger on "ol Madam'. Come on now, we're gonna be late for supper."

By sunset, the ongoing routines had mostly taken the edge off of things. Grandpa had gone about his own quiet investigation. Trusting that he had trained me well, he looked for the explanation that must be there. My cousin Will, he discovered, had loaded the gun after I had cleaned it and set it out for target practice while he put on his boots. He thought I was taking the Stevens double barrel, he said, and he had cleaned that for me.

"You don't leave a loaded gun around even long enough to get your shoes on, William," my grandfather chided Will as my cousin looked at me with daggers. Got me in trouble again you little brat, his eyes said.

Mr. Laveen, the local Game Warden/Postmaster, came and confiscated the bird, shaking his head and still scolding my grandfather as he turned his car around in the yard. There had been no fine, no prison sentence. Just a lot of disgusted looks in my direction and then a few jokes about enjoying a little duck and wild rice in early July as he was waved off down the long driveway.

I was sitting on the porch watching the rose and amber clouds the setting sun had left behind. Lewis was asleep at my feet, or pretending to be, and I absently picked the burrs from his legs. I heard the screen door creak open as Grandpa came out to take his usual place on the bench against the wall. My father had left for his office in the Twin Cities for a few days. He had hugged me and whispered encouragingly, "Don't make over much of it, Johnny. The feelings will pass."

He smiled and waved as he left and I smiled back. I watched the sun fade and waited for the feelings to go away. The smoke of Grandpa's cigar drifted past me and tangled itself in the lilac bushes.

"There won't be a whole lot of times left for us to

hunt together after this Fall, young man. We better make the best of it."

I looked back, shocked not so much by the thought as by the fact that he was talking about it.

"Oh, I don't mean I've got one foot in the grave or anything, so don't look so glum. We've got some time left for sure. But, one of these days, Johnny, your old grandpa is going to slip quietly off to his Maker. You gotta remember, it's all in the cycle of things. Everything comes to an end. This farm. The people you love. Lewis there. Most people don't like to think about it. But, you see, that doesn't help one bit. Life is a wonderful thing, at least it has been for me, but it doesn't make any sense at all without death being a part of it. There's an old Irish saying, 'If I fill up with enough life while I'm here I may have enough left over to take with me'. Nonsense, of course, like most Irish sayings, but a comfort to some."

It was always very quiet on the farm in the evening. We sat in the stillness, my grandfather and I, with our own thoughts and the day passing away. I knew he had meant to make me feel better about the duck. But my feelings had nothing to do with that kind of death. For the first time in my life, I was struck by the thought that I had killed something. Because of a game, I had torn life out of the summer sky. I had done it, just as I had before, because of the mad excitement it had given me. Chance had not taken a life. Nature had not taken her course. I had killed and that feeling would never pass.

CHAPTER IV

A nod is as good as a wink
to a blind horse

Lynn came up from the creek, the lower pasture laid out green and silent over her shoulder. I sat on the rusted seat of the old McCormick tractor behind the corn crib, where I had come to contemplate my future and watched her as though through a wide angle lens, her forward motion distorted so that her approach seemed endless. She was held in space like the 'twir' of the meadowlark off to her left. I had always thought of her as Richard's sister. They were the only two close to our age within easy walking distance, so my sister and I spent most of our summers in their company. The four of us had grown up together, but Richard was three years older than I and was now taking over much of the work on his father's farm. I saw him less and less each summer. Her name might have been Jane or Sue or Sally for, as far as I was concerned, she was just a girl.

On this particular morning I studied her approach and something stirred inside me. I shifted position on the seat and fiddled with the throttle lever. When I looked up, she had stopped by the front of the tractor, both hands pushed into the back pockets of her baggy jeans. She kicked at the old front wheel.

"Where's Patty, anyway?"

"Dunno," I said, "I think she went to town with Mom. Where's Richard?"

"Raking prob'ly." She shaded her eyes against the sun behind me. "Down by the lake, I think. What are you doin'?"

I shrugged and went back to moving the throttle up and down. Even now, whenever a woman looks at me and asks me a direct question, I tend to look away. Once, in my early twenties, I had forced myself to look straight into the green eyes of a woman who asked me if I loved her. I did not turn away and finally she dropped her head. "Of course I love you," I had said. Perhaps she knew that I had spoken to the empty space beyond her or, perhaps, she believed that my eyes had not wavered. I knew.

"My father bought me a flute," Lynn said. "It's silver. I'm going to play in the band this Fall." She was standing on the front wheel of the tractor with her arms spread like a tight rope walker's and she was smiling. There was a single drop of perspiration sliding down her right cheek. I watched as it was about to drop off the side of her chin, but she reached absently across with the back of her left hand and brushed it away.

"Do you wanna go down to the lake?" she said.

"Na, I just ate."

"What's that got to do with going to the lake? We could give Richie a bad time."

"Na."

"C'mon, it's hot just sittin' here."

I slid off the seat and started off down the fence line that led to the lake dividing her father's farm from ours. She skipped past me and turned around to face me, skip-stepping backwards with her hands again in her back pockets.

"We could go skinny dippin'. Nobody'd be around by the rope."

Skinny dippin' with Lynn was like skinny dippin' with any other friend, except she was as strong as an ox, a real tomboy. She always dunked me under and one of these times I knew she would drown me for sure. But it was hot and the thought of arching out over the cool of Lake Cullen, letting go of the rope, and plummeting feet first into its freshness was nice.

A long time before, someone had tied a big rope to a sturdy limb of the single oak tree that shaded Cullen's west bank in the afternoon. The four of us had added an old gunny sack filled with rags and knotted it to the end of the rope. We would pull the sack back as far as it would go, then run for the end of the bank. When we reached the drop off, we would fling ourselves out to the sack and glide out and up into the leaves and the sky. One giant yell would carry us up to the end of the rope, the rush of hot air against our faces as we were lifted beyond the shade. We were held there for an instant, the rope pulled taut.

I could see the whole afternoon in that instant. The endless blue of the sky against green-gold fields smelling new mown. The older men working like ants moving across the fields on their little toy wagons. The lone spire of St. Canice topping a clump of green that was Kilkerry. As the rope began to slacken I unfolded my legs, held the rope from falling back for just a moment, then dropped down hearing Lynn squeal on the bank and then my own shriek turning to a gurgle as I sank into the silent coolness. As I propelled myself back to the surface, Lynn was already in the air. I turned on my back to watch as I pushed toward shore. She was out and up, way beyond the leaves, and as the rope's length gave out, she was caught in a golden flash that came above the tree. The sack was twisted so that she was facing me. She unfolded her legs and as she held the rope above her for a moment, she was bronzed in a dancer's tableau that ripped at my stomach and constricted my throat.

There was no explanation in my mind for such a feeling, no understanding beyond the sudden confusion that churned in my stomach. I was to remember that feeling in later years when I understood what it meant and what I might do about it. Yet, now I wonder if indeed I have ever felt quite the same thing with as much intensity.

By the time she came giggling out of the water, I had pulled on my jeans and was lying on my back in the clean warmth of the bank. Swinging and swimming in the nude was as ordinary for us as it was for most to wear bathing suits. Out of some intuitive sense of modesty, however, we never lay sprawled in our nakedness on the shore. Actually, it was probably based on more practical reasons like comfort, protection from ants, a way to dry off, or maybe even a place to put our hands more than out of any sense of modesty.

I heard rather than saw her wiggle into her jeans and lay beside me in the grass. I was looking directly at the point where she had been held captive by the sun for that moment and I did not want to look at her now. She knows, I thought. She knows what happened, but won't tell me. She will laugh if I let her see that I am confused, that I don't know what she knows. I was convinced even then that Lynn was the cause of what I had felt. More than that, she had done something, engineered something, that was designed to hurt me or upset me.

I could hear her next to me. I wanted her to go up there again so I could test my theory. I wanted to see her stretched, both hands holding the sky, shining there in midair so unreal. I wanted to see her up there again because I was not sure now that it had really been her. I did not want to look at her next to me. I was afraid. I knew it, though I wasn't sure why. I also knew just as surely that I could never, ever tell anyone, especially Lynn Galvin.

We had been quiet for a long time. Lynn pulled a tufted weed, put it in her mouth and, turning on her side, tickled inside my ear. As I flicked my arm to get rid of what I thought was a fly, she giggled and said between clenched teeth, "What'cha thinkin'?"

I turned to face her and passed from being afraid to being terrified. Out of the lump in my throat

I croaked, "Can I see it sometime?"

She took the weed slowly out of her mouth and smiled down into the grass. "See what?"

"The flute, the silver flute or whatever."

She rolled over on her back and twirled the weed like a baton over her head. "Maybe. Maybe sometime at school."

"Why not before school?   What's the big deal anyway?"

"It's no big deal. I just don't want to take it all over the place and get it wrecked."

~ ~ ~ ~

I was not aware that any great changes had taken place in me over the last year, but there was no mistaking the change in the girl who looked into my frightened eyes. I didn't know much about boys and girls or men and women, but I did know that she was different from the girl I had seen the summer before. I wasn't a complete dummy. I knew that girls grew breasts. My sister was two years older than I was and she had breasts, at least she liked to claim she did. I used to kid her about her bra being made by Johnson and Johnson. Her feminine pride would bring an anger into her huge brown eyes that had me running for my life, trying to keep my feet moving while I doubled over with laughter.

I didn't expect Lynn to have breasts. As she lay on her back, they were hardly perceptible but the image of her at the end of the rope only moments ago was frozen in my mind. She was just one year older than I was, but she had sensed a change in herself and she was testing out her womanhood. I suspected she knew that my heart was racing and she liked the power of being responsible for that.

~ ~ ~ ~

"Jackie, have you ever kissed a girl?"

A lumpy bullfrog hopped onto a mud pile and stared pop-eyed at the sweat collecting on my forehead. His white throat pulsated up and down and I knew he was saying just what I was saying to myself. "Go ahead, stupid, tell her the truth and see how smug she gets." The frog knew. Lynn probably knew, too. I lay back and let my breath out between my lips with what I hoped was a disgusted whoosh.

"What do you think?"

I didn't know then that women have a finely tuned sense of when a man is cornered. On reflection, I sometimes think about how unfair it is that this same sense should be instilled in young girls at the expense of boys still limping toward puberty.

"You never have, have you?" She absently picked the kernels from the end of the weed.

"I have so, lots of times. Millie O'Grady for one." I was pretty smart to pick Millie because even if Lynn asked her, Millie had kissed so many boys she wouldn't remember them all. Besides, I had come real close one time with Millie anyway, but I had to go to the bathroom and by the time I returned the recess bell had rung and we had to go back to class. I knew, however, that this was different, that kissing Lynn would not be the same as kissing Millie O'Grady. I was frightened but I was also filled with a strange kind of anticipation. Somewhere in the cloudy part of my understanding, I knew I had been waiting for something like this. Not this girl maybe and not this very thing, but something like this.

~ ~ ~ ~

I remember when I was very young my cousin would take me with him to the pasture to catch the horses. I would look up at him, as I skipped along to keep up and wonder if I could ever be like him. We would both carry a lead rope and snapping them against our legs we would cluck the usual "comealong" sounds. "Here boy, easy now, that a boy, over here girl." When we finally coaxed them to us, sometimes using a few oats to seduce them, we would fix the rope around their strong necks as we patted them firmly. My cousin had cautioned me many times about petting and stroking a horse.

"They're not like dogs," he told me, "you have to strike them with your open hand hard on the flank or the neck, never stroke their nose, and brush them hard with a curry or brush. They like that. Hit yourself first on the thigh before you pat them so they know they are getting equal treatment."

When they were settled down and ready to take up to the barn my cousin would mount one of them and, after I had handed him the other lead, he would pull me up behind him. We repeated that same routine for a long time until one morning, when my cousin was mounted, instead of handing the lead rope for the other horse, I simply grabbed the long white mane and threw myself up across his neck. Why at that particular time, I can't explain, except that in that instant something told me it was time. My cousin simply looked back over his shoulder and said, "You lead."

Somehow deep within us preparations are forever taking place. Preparations for our first independent move, for our first fistfight, for our first Lynn Galvin. I suspect now that Lynn was a slight bit better prepared than I on that summer yesterday.

~   ~   ~   ~

I yanked off my jeans and headed for the lake to clear my head and to avoid the challenge to my claim of having kissed Millie. I swam free of the shade that had now extended further into the lake so that I could feel at once the cool water sliding around me and the prick of the late afternoon sun on my back. Suddenly, she was on me. I found myself flailing and sputtering under water. The sun penetrated in diffused shafts broken by our two bodies twisting and tumbling in a confusion of limbs.

The game was old and familiar. I could deal with it much better than the new one that seemed to be intruding on my childhood. We kicked and jostled, screamed and threatened until we were paddling about like tired retrievers just barely able to make the shore. We collapsed, heaving and gasping far more than was necessary, and coughed out promises of revenge. By the time our breathing had returned to normal, we were again on our backs but the tension was gone and there were no more questions about my accomplishments with girls.

Neither of us had put on our jeans this time. As we lay drying in the sun, I could sense her next to me and I turned up on one elbow to look at her. I wanted to touch her. I simply wanted to reach over and touch this new experience. I felt that perhaps it would bring something into focus, that the sensation might provide me with some kind of key that would unlock the mystery that edged its way into my afternoon. I lay immobile as she curled to a sitting position and pulled on her jeans, turned her back to me and clasped her bra. I was unable to change my position or to put on my own clothes. I was overcome with an empty feeling that something had just slipped through my grasp and that I would never again be able to recapture it, never. The sense of loss I felt was overwhelming, made even more distressing because I had no idea what it was exactly that I was losing.

Lynn turned toward me and, at least in my perception, looked directly at me as she slowly picked up her shirt, carefully buttoned each button up the front, rose, then stood looking down at me for what seemed like an hour, then headed up the fence line for home.

"Aren't you coming, Jackie? I'm gonna be late for chores."

"Ya, I'm comin'." I hopped around trying to rush into my pants and shirt and scurried after her like a little puppy dog, only my tail was not wagging. "What's wrong? Did I do something wrong? Slow down, we got lots of time."

I watched her straight back continue to move away from me and finally I slowed down and kicked at some dirt clumps. I saw her dip into the creek bed and up the other side and then she was gone. All the familiar sounds of the fields and the woods fogged into a blur. I didn't see or hear anything. I was numb. By the time I realized I was crying I was sitting in a heap by the lug wheel of the old McCormick tractor.

CHAPTER V

The older the fiddle
the sweeter the tune

Death comes to visit us, I believe, long before we actually take our last sweet breath.   He begins to invade the space around us and the fetid smell of him infects not only the air, but those who breathe it as well. Perhaps he comes only to wait, empty- eyed and horrible in his unseen presence.   Or, perhaps, given some slight crack of weakness in the wall of human dimension, he slips in to quicken the end. If he came thinking to whisk my great aunts away into his black and empty world, he must have been exasperated and fuming with impatience.   The worldweary yet somehow sadly gallant trio would have none of his interference. They took their own sweet time.

~ ~ ~ ~

My aunts Jane, Margreg, and Bridey had found themselves unmarried long after the time when any eligible young man might consider seeking their hands in marriage. Sickness partially, but mostly self pity and a lack of purpose, led them in later years to take up residence in what was once our front parlor. It remained a bright and cheerful room for a while. The sunshine and the moonlight dancing off the lawn and the fields kept their dreams and misguided hopes alive. Perhaps they even giggled and teased when they were alone, just as they had when the Judge was alive and their lives were full of promise. But gradually the room darkened, closed up, and took the shape of their bitter hearts. What joy remained sometimes showed itself in the corners of Aunt Bridey's eyes or in the girlish swing of Aunt Margreg's feet dangling off the side of her unmade bed. But these were only occasional and quickly lost to the emptiness that sucked it away. Three colorful and beautiful flowers were dying in the darkness.

~ ~ ~ ~

Once each day, like everyone else in the family, I was expected to enter this world and visit "The Aunties." It must have been an uncomfortable experience for the adults. It was terribly painful for me. Like all the other children, I would seize on any excuse to avoid this daily visitation. Like all of the others, too, I was seldom successful. One afternoon that summer I rapped lightly on the door to their room, secretly hoping they would be asleep and not hear me.

"I tried this afternoon," I would tell my mother, "but they must have been asleep or didn't feel like company."

With luck, she would be too busy to insist that I

try again.   It had worked before.   But, on this particular afternoon, my luck did not hold.   My Aunt Jane was actually out of bed and rather than the usual feeble, "Yes, come in," she opened the door herself and stood aside to let me enter. She was in unusually good spirits. She walked in front of me, her slippered feet moving almost lightly across the floor and sent me to my usual chair with a wave of her cane. "Jackie, Jackie," she was saying with more energy than I had felt in this room in almost two years, "I am so glad you came to visit us just now, we all are really. Goodness me, yes, this is a real treat, Jackie."

Jane was the oldest of my grandfather's three sisters.   Like the others, she had been a school teacher but before that she had been Judge Thomas Laney's beautiful and eligible young daughter.   She was, like all my great aunts, a tiny woman but she was Irish to the core and full of what my Uncle Shay called "spit and vinegar." Some of that spirit was still left in the old maid I watched excitedly go about the room opening drapes and windows. Dark brown liver spots covered her hands, neck, and face and showed in the space between slippers and hem. The substance of her had dropped away so that the skin was drawn tight against her bones or fell in wrinkled folds that jiggled when she moved. Shadows under her gray-blue eyes hid the fire that had once both warmed and frightened her students. She was, on most days, very weak, her voice a whisper, her face an ashen gray. Today she had found some hidden reserves to call upon, for she chattered endlessly as she moved about the room. She carried a blackthorn walking stick that now stands in my front hall, but she was barely using it now except to gesture with or to move a drape aside.

My Aunt Margreg was sitting in an old oak straight-backed chair with little bits of stuffing and burlap webbing hanging beneath its leather-covered seat. Someone, probably my mother, had helped her into a dress she could not have worn for years for there was not a time in my memory when The Aunties had left their room. Poking out from under her lacy dress were two white and puffy ankles stuck incongruously into a large pair of men's bedroom slippers. Her thinning hair had been brushed and done up in a small bun at the nape of her neck. Her hands rested quietly in her lap, but her eyes were dancing with delight and one toe tapped softly on the floor as if to the beat of some unheard music.

Aunt Bridey, entirely confined to her bed, was propped up with her pillows. She wore a white cotton cap on her head and I suspected she was almost completely bald, although I had never thought to ask if this were true. She was fidgeting with the linen shawl wrapped about her shoulders, the blue-veined and bony fingers adjusting and readjusting it closer around her neck. The room was stuffy and warm with the July heat, but perhaps she felt a chill the rest of us were not aware of. Her tiny head moved uncontrollably from side to side in double time to the ticking of the old clock that stood just inside the door. She could not turn her head all the way toward me but she was watching me with her eyes and smiling. What teeth she had left were stained and worn almost to the gums but it was a beautiful smile.

This was not to be my usual visit to The Aunties. On other occasions, all three would be in bed, the curtains drawn, not a breath of air stirring, my own entrance the only movement. The few questions and answers would be carried on in whispers, interspersed with much coughing and moans of discomfort. Today was unusual. Something had sparked these three old ladies into life and I had come knocking at just the right moment. Finished with the windows, Aunt Jane now paced back and forth in front of her bed striking the walking stick against the floor at each turn like a punctuation mark. Nobody spoke. When I started to ask a question, Aunt Jane put a hairy finger to her lips and went on pacing. Aunt Margreg rocked and Aunt Bridey fidgeted and the clock ticked.

The knocking startled me. At Jane's bidding, my Aunt Mary entered carrying a large silver tray. The tray was laden with pastries, a cold pitcher of lemonade and several glasses. We all watched as she placed the tray on the table nearest Aunt Jane's bed. When she turned to go she asked, "Will there be anything else, Jane?"

"No, no this will be just fine, thank you dear."

"I brought an extra glass," my Aunt Mary said as she was leaving, "I thought Jackie might be joining you." She gave me a broad wink and left. The door closed quietly behind and I thought that now I would discover the mystery of this strange transformation. But still my Aunt Jane paced. Aunt Bridey's head and the ticking clock began to get me confused, I would start to get the rhythm of one and the other would throw me off completely.   Aunt Margreg tapped to a rhythm in her head and Aunt Jane's stick tapped counter punctually to every other sound.   Just as I thought perhaps I should make some comment and prepare to leave, the clock struck four o'clock and all three sisters stopped their respective movements and looked at the old Seth Thomas by the door.

"Today is my birthday, Jackie."

I turned to look at my Aunt Margreg.   "I didn't know that Aunt Margreg," I said, "I would have brought you something."

"Oh, my that isn't necessary, Jackie.   I'm far too old for gifts and sentimental cards.   They tend to last longer than we do anyway and that's too sad.   Memories.   Now they last just long enough.   They're gone when we are."

I think it was more than I had ever heard my aunt say at any one time and I looked at her tapping her toe and realized that for all the days I had come here to visit, I didn't know these women at all. I knew little of the history, only bits and pieces put together from many conversations.   I knew even less of their cares and feelings.

"It isn't really her birthday," Aunt Jane said going to the rocker and adjusting a wisp of her sister's hair. "Nobody really knows the exact date, but it is her baptismal day and that is close enough, isn't it dear?"

"We're going to have a party," Bridey said as she reached a frail hand in my direction, "Come, sit by me now so we can begin.   If Jane doesn't pour our lemonade soon, I'll fall asleep and miss the whole affair."

"Well, my yes, it's four o'clock and so now we can have our little party."

"Why four o'clock, Aunt Jane? Was that the time of the baptism?"

"Goodness no," Aunt Margreg said, "Baptisms are always in the morning, don't you know.   Saturday mornings.   Confessions are heard on Saturday afternoons."

"The Judge, your great-grandfather, always said a successful party started at four o'clock," Jane said as she poured the lemonade. I was amazed that she had gotten that right because most of the time she wasn't certain whether I was my father, my uncle, one of my cousins, or myself.   She splashed and spilled the lemonade into the glasses and asked if I would serve one to each of us. Then she went on.

"Oh," she sighed, her eyes brightly twinkling in spite of her frailty.   "Oh, the parties this room has seen, Jackie, you would be surprised."   She almost floated across the room as she explained, gesturing first with her stick and then with her free hand. "The Judge would invite people from several counties, the room would be filled with people and music...."

"And color," interrupted Bridey.

"Yes, and color, and fresh air drifting in from the doors that used to open here onto the veranda.   It was a gay and wonderful time then," she stopped to take the lemonade I offered, "and, of course we were just girls."

"Were you very sick then, too?" I asked realizing too late how impolite that was.

For the first time I could remember, my Aunt

Jane laughed. Aunt Bridey covered her mouth with a corner of her shawl and giggled softly and Aunt Margreg dribbled lemonade down the front of her dress. The youthfulness of their laughter infected me and I laughed too and the room grew bright like the afternoon sun.

"My goodness no," Aunt Margreg coughed as she wiped at her bosom with her hanky. "My goodness, no. We were all strong and healthy. Part of the strength of this farm. Your Aunt Bridey was the prettiest, and Jane the most popular."

Aunt Bridey's head stopped for just a moment in the surety of her conviction. "But you were the best dancer, Margreg, you were always the best dancer."

"I did love to dance. Such beautiful music and so many nice young boys and so much time, Jackie, so much time to enjoy it all. I remember my sixteenth birthday best of all." She stopped for a moment staring past me through the open doors that were not there any longer. I heard Jane sigh and Bridey leaned back against her pillows and repeated, "Yes, yes," very softly several times.

"It was on this very day, July 10th, because it was my baptismal day. It was almost four o'clock and I spent all day getting ready."

"Getting dressed was not so simple then, Jackie." Aunt Bridey offered and she giggled again behind her shawl.

"I hadn't been in the front parlor yet, but I knew what it would look like. The little chocolate cakes that mother would make and my favorite strawberry tarts and, of course, the cold apple cider and fresh lemonade all set out on the veranda where it was shady and cool. The Judge would have insisted on fresh flowers and a special Birthday Bouquet as a centerpiece. It would be lovely, I knew."

"And you were lovely too, dear, wasn't she, Bridey?" Aunt Jane added.

I thought my Aunt Bridey had dozed off but she had been listening and remembering too. "Yes, yes," she purred. "You were lovely too Margreg."

Aunt Margreg's eyes had begun to fill with tears and she was about to drop her glass. I took it from her hands and set it to one side. Aunt Jane shook her head and led me to the foot of Aunt Bridey's bed again, using her walking stick more now, she shuffled to her sister's side and asked her gently if she would like to return to bed. Aunt Margreg shook her head and patted Aunt Jane's hand.

"My goodness no, Janey, this is my party and we still have tarts to eat and music, too. Are we going to have music, Janey?"

"Well, perhaps later, dear." She shuffled back to refill her lemonade glass. After a moment Aunt Margreg continued as if she had never stopped.

"And music, Jackie, there was always such beautiful music. This party would be special, though," she pointed her finger toward me wanting me to understand. "This would be our first party with the new Gramophone. The Judge had brought it from Chicago and we were to dance to its music for the first time at my party. I was to have the first dance with my father, then all the young beaus would line up to take their turns. After they danced with Jane, of course, that was only proper."   Here she actually winked at me.

"Yes, that's true and then I would be last," Aunt Bridey added.

"But not least," said Aunt Jane, "certainly not least, Bridey."

"What kind of dancing did you do, Aunt Margreg?" I asked. "I don't know how."

"Why, Jackie, you mean you have never danced? Never, ever?"   She was genuinely shocked.   "My goodness, a young man must know how to dance. Mustn't he Jane?"

"Why of course." Aunt Jane said, the twinkle coming again to her eyes.

"Yes, yes." Aunt Bridey added.

"Why don't you have a sweet now, Jackie. They are your Aunt Margreg's favorite tarts. Go ahead now, help yourself."

The little pie crust shells had been filled with ripe strawberries and covered with fresh whipped cream. I knew my Aunt Mary must have made them especially for the occasion because I had never seen them before.   I started to take one and then remembered my manners and lifted the tray to offer one to my Aunts. Aunt Margreg said maybe later, Aunt Jane took one and set it on a napkin in her lap, but Aunt Bridey said,

"No, I mustn't.   A bedpan is a most uncomfortable thing and I try to use it as little as possible. Sweet things tend to make…"

There was an embarrassed cough from Aunt Jane, but Bridey went right on, "Your father offered to put a real bathroom in for us with running water and everything, but these two old ladies can't be bothered with such a modern convenience. When I think of how much more comfortable a bowel..."

"Really, Bridget." Aunt Jane interrupted. "Jackie is not interested in your preoccupation with bodily functions. Now have another sweet, Jackie, before the cream turns in this heat."

Aunt Margreg was still with her memories, thinking of times when time was unimportant and moments were gathered like flowers.

"We did many different dances, but my favorite was the waltz, of course. I danced the first dance with Father and it was beautiful played on the new Gramophone. Come, take my arm and I'll teach you, Jackie."

My Aunt Jane was at her side before I could get there, concern on her face. Aunt Bridey, too, had propped herself up, her shawl falling from her shoulders as she protested,

"Now, now Margreg you mustn't, dear, the time has gone quickly and Jackie must get back to his chores."

But Aunt Margreg was already on her feet supporting herself between Aunt Jane and me.

"Nonsense, we can't have a birthday party without dancing. Just a few steps and then our time will be up."

"But we have no music, dear." Aunt Jane said.

"No matter. The steps are what is most important for a young man to learn."

With a courage and elegance supported by her

memories, she moved slowly to the middle of the room and began a box step counting out loud, "One, two, three. One, two, three." She looked toward me and motioned me to follow her steps.   I was embarrassed and intrigued all at once but gradually I was caught up in her concentration. Her slippered feet moved lightly over the floor as her voice picked up a musical sound and she encouraged me to find the rhythm.   Then she stopped, straightened herself up, put her right hand out to the side, and lifted her skirt with her left.

"Now," she said with authority, "a young man must always stand straight and tall, his hands must be firm but gentle. Put your left hand in mine and your right hand just above my waist. There, you see?"

I did as she said and nodded but was not at all sure what to do next.

"Now count with me. One, two, three...."

We began with the simple box step.   I was amazed at how light she felt as we moved across the floor. She neither faltered nor stumbled but held her head high as she guided me into a long sweeping turn. She began to hum softly a melody I had never heard and soon Aunt Jane and Aunt Bridey, too, were humming with her as we twirled about the room. The evening sun slanted across us and lit the blush on her girlish face as she smiled up at me and hummed the music of a time gone by. She stumbled slightly when the clock struck five, but we finished our turn until the song ended.   She stepped away and taking the wrinkled dress in her hands she curtsied and said,

"I thank you sir. You are a fine dancer."

I bowed the way I had seen in movies and said, "My pleasure, Miss Margreg."

She smiled then and Jane and Bridey were smiling and so was I. And death, sitting in a shadowed corner nearby must have been a bit confused. Perhaps Grandpa had been right that evening on the back porch. Perhaps all things do come to an end. But it wasn't time for these three quite yet. My Great Aunt Margreg was able to hold him at bay until late that winter. When she died, I suppose I cried. But I can never, to this day, begin a dance without remembering that lady in my arms.

CHAPTER VI

As the old cock crows
the young cock learns

When a Minnesota summer burns itself into July, something of a strange stillness invades the rural landscape and the people who populate it.   Most everything has finished growing and seems to simply settle into ripening under a white sky. Movement, too, slows as if the world were weighted down by the damp heat. The few token thunderheads that nature offers seem somehow reluctant to move, piling up on the horizon for days before, almost with an effort, they crawl across the sky and gratuitously drop their collected moisture onto an already saturated world. Time as well creeps across the summer sky suspending its descent in huge red brilliance. It is, of course, expected and passes with all but an occasional comment. My grandfather used to say it was a time that tested the character of a people, my mother said it characterized a testy people, and the old timers in

Kilkerry said it was good for the corn. Yet, every once in while, an even greater stillness comes into such a summer day. A kind of stillness that denies not only movement, but sound as well.

"When such a quiet comes," my grandfather told me, "when the birds are quiet and the bugs are quiet and not a blade of grass stirs, the one thing that better be moving is your feet."

~ ~ ~ ~

On such a July day, and not too early in the morning because there were chores to be done, my cousin William and I and a rather obnoxious friend, Melvin, slipped off to go fishing in Cow Creek. Very few fish were ever caught in Cow Creek. Some called it a river, but even though the halfhearted little stream twisted its way through half a dozen counties and in and out of numerous lakes, it never managed to exceed the status of creek in my mind. Once in a great while, we would snag an unsuspecting catfish and lug it home for my aunt to fry up for our lunch. But more often our lines were cast and withdrawn only to be studiously reset every half hour or so in what the patient angler sensed as a more likely spot. We always went with a full can of fresh worms or, perhaps, a bit of bacon rind, but no more than a single worm per hook was ever used. Fishing was not what we were about.

I found out several years later what real fishing was about when I began fly fishing with my father. What we did at Cow Creek was stay cool in the shade, avoid work, and discuss the weighty questions of life. "Pondering," my cousin Will called it. We pondered this and we pondered that and all the while the creek slid by in silence as it had for our fathers before us and for their fathers, too, and the morning sun climbed to noon or just past.

Will usually decided the topic we would ponder or maybe, if something had crossed my mind, I might ask if we could ponder that for a while. On this particular day nothing was on my mind and Will seemed content to simply let the time pass. It was Melvin who got us going on the subject of sex. I don't think I had pondered that subject much in the past, but I surprised myself by how quickly I perked up at the suggestion. I had tried not to think too much about Lynn Galvin and had avoided her whenever possible. When Will claimed to have some knowledge on the subject, I got real antsy and jabbed myself with my fishhook. The subject seemed to be painful in more ways than one. I was about to suggest a different topic, but Will claimed it was a subject that could be pondered at great length and that it was just the thing we should be talking about even if the choice had been Melvin's.

Melvin Hobson was a tagalong. He had no friends, at least that I was aware of, which I found perfectly understandable. He had tiny little eyes sunk in a pudgy baby face that was covered with pimples. Melvin attacked each new blemish with a vengeance every time he faced a mirror. The resulting wounds gave him the appearance of someone just recovering from the chicken pox. The rest of his body was stuck onto his head like a Mr. Potato. The whole effect would have been comic if he were not so entirely obnoxious and offensive. Just as my family was generally soft spoken and basically gentle in their language, Melvin's family was loud, coarse, and generally crass in not only their language, but in their behavior as well.

"For all of that," my grandfather would say, "the Hobsons run a fine farm and are generous neighbors. Old man Hobson may cuss and fume when he stubs his toe, but he speaks gently to his wife. And Melvin may have a bit of a foul mouth, but he never misses giving his respects to the adults and he has a quiet way with your sister."

Melvin and my sister would be a hard combination to understand but, then, there seemed to be lots of things I didn't understand when it came to relationships. It was true about Melvin I suppose. He had his nice side. However, it made him no more pleasant to be with the majority of the time. Especially when he got to telling some of the filthiest jokes I have heard even to this day. So I wasn't surprised when from just below me on the bank I heard him say,

"My sister-in-law, Clara, popped another kid last night. Damn near dropped it on the kitchen floor before they could get her into the front room."

"Was it a boy or a girl?" I asked, genuinely pleased for his sister.

"It was definitely a boy. Typical Hobson wang, sittin' straight up and ready for action."

While Melvin related the story of the late night birth, complete with graphic details of the pain and blood and visual images of his sister-in-law's anatomy,

I lay back and watched a thankful breeze wind through the old willow we sat beneath. Will pulled his line out and carefully examined the night crawler that was still wrigglin' on his hook. Every once in awhile, he would look at Melvin with disgust or shake his head in disbelief.

I had seen lots of animals born. Often, I would keep vigil for days hoping to have the opportunity to help my father or Uncle Shay pull a calf or I would lie peering through the bottom slat of a pen for hours waiting to see an old sow give birth to her piglets. There had even been a number of tragedies, stillbirths, and one colt that was terribly deformed. All the adults and my older cousins were willing to answer any and all questions. It was part of what you needed to know on a farm. I had never seen or heard about the birth of a baby. I had imagined it was much the same. Melvin's description, however, seemed to be what Will later called "sexier." I wanted to be disgusted like my older and more mature cousin, but I found myself listening with more interest than I thought I should. I didn't want to have to talk about this with Fr. Shea, our parish priest, on Saturday afternoon in the confessional. But I felt those ugly pangs of good old Irish Catholic guilt and tried not to listen to the vulgar narrative of Clara Hobson's delivery. The wind had begun to bend the branches and I noticed Will occasionally glancing out across the meadow to the cornfields rolling in multiple shades of green before the coming storm. I was about to suggest we start for the house before the rain came when Melvin turned over his shoulder and challenged,

"I bet you don't even know how babies get started, do ya Laney?"

I was startled because the truth was, I didn't. I mean, I had my suspicions, but they were unclear and certainly untested. I looked to my cousin and he must have seen the confusion on my face, because he came to my assistance. He played his line out to the middle of the creek, leaned his long back against the bank and said,

"I suppose you do, huh, Hobson?" Even at sixteen, Will was developing the skills of a teacher. He was expert at asking questions and leading the direction of our "ponderings."

"Course I know." He gave me a cavity-filled leer and said, "But you don't, do ya?"

"I know as much as you do," I snapped and pulled my line out from under the roots it had drifted into.

"Ya, it's pretty simple," he went on determined to share his wisdom. "Ya just stick the old wanger in, take a pee and Nature mixes the juices all together and starts a kid, right, Will?"

Will sat up and looked at him with loathing. My mouth dropped open and I stared with unbelieving eyes at the cousin who could clarify all this. Before Will could answer, Melvin went right on.

"You've seen your Daddy's bull do it, Laney. Stick that old two foot wang in there. Well, that's the way it's done. Same thing with horses and pigs and you and me, 'cept we got a lot less to work with."

"Why don't you shut up, Hobson?" Will had stood up and was standing over Melvin with anger flashing in his eyes.

"Hey, what is it with you? I'm right and you know it. I know what I know. I saw you and......"

Will's foot came up so fast I barely saw it. It caught Melvin just below the chin and snapped his head back against the bank. Melvin curled up in a ball and rocked back and forth while my cousin William glared down at him, every muscle in his six foot frame tight as a spring. I barely noticed the groans and curses coming from the ground as I stared dumbfounded at my cousin. I didn't know whether I was more shocked by what I had heard or at the unexpected violent reaction of Will. William, who could calm a panicked horse with a single word or with a gentle touch. William, who laid his forehead against a nervous cow until she'd give more milk than even my Uncle Shay could command.

All was still except for the muffled sounds from Melvin. It was so quiet I could hear my own rapid breathing. It was too quiet. The willow was no longer moving and the kingfisher that had been darting up and down the creek had disappeared. Will sensed it just as I did and turned three hundred and sixty degrees looking at the sky.

"The root cellar!" I yelled and dropping my pole I pulled on Melvin trying to get him to his feet but he was still curled up rocking back and forth and moaning,

"Jesus God, Jesus God."

"Tornado!" I screamed. "Tornado, Hobson, we gotta make the root cellar."

"Too late," Will mumbled and pushed me up the

bank.

"Hobson!" I yelled as I scrambled up to the meadow.

"Leave him," Will hissed and pushed me again.

We stood at the edge of the meadow and I was suddenly gripped by a fear I had never felt before. A world without sound or movement is spellbinding and I found myself unable to move. The blackness that moved up over the horizon thrust forth a shadow that crawled across the ground with a stalking life of its own.

"Move!" Will shouted, even though there was no need to raise his voice.

"Where?"

"The road, where the creek goes under."

"What?"

"The culvert! Move!" he shouted again.

Remembering my grandfather's warning then, I began to run with Will ahead of me. I looked once over my shoulder and saw Melvin stumble into the field and follow us. By the time we reached the culvert, the sky was totally black and great drops of rain had soaked us to the skin. The wind tore at us from every direction and suddenly the noise was deafening. I don't remember how long we huddled there, calf deep in the water, as the storm hurled itself in full fury at everything in its path. It was impossible to see beyond the dark and the rain and even if we shouted, the words were lost to the storm.

We were left to our own thoughts and our own fears. We had no idea where the storm would touch down nor how many times, but we knew it was close.

The destruction it caused was always astounding and there was always a sigh of relief if one escaped the full force of it.   I thought of the men who had been working far from the house and the unprotected livestock and the women who would be huddled in the root cellar thinking, in turn, about their men and about us.   I found myself thinking about my mother and father and, unbidden, about the things Melvin had said.   I thought about my sister and my cousin, Vanessa, and wondered if they were safe and if someday a man would...or if already...I looked at Melvin rotating his chin and working his jaw up and down and suddenly I hoped that it was broken.

The storm was over just as suddenly as it had come. Will was the first one out of the culvert. I saw him standing up on the road looking toward the house.

"Is everything O.K.?" I asked, trying to keep my voice calm.

"Can't see anybody and the barn looks funny. Hard to tell from here, but it seems O.K."

We both started out across the field when I heard Melvin up on the road.

"I better get my butt home too," he said.

"Ya, we'll see ya later.   Hope everything's all right."

He nodded and started off.   Will didn't say anything. I watched his back and tried to equal his long stride as I wondered who he really was.   He hadn't said anything to Hobson and he wasn't saying much to me.

"So why did you kick Melvin, anyway? What did he see ya do, Will?"

"None of your business."   He snapped and then he added, "You're too young, ya know."

"Jeeze," I mumbled.   I hated it when someone said that, although in later years I would hear myself say it many times.   I never saw myself as too young to hear anything and then somebody would say something and I would wish I'd never asked.

"Cripes, Will, I'm not too young," I said as I scrambled up to his side.   "I started the tractor and your dad said I was old enough to do anything."

Will stopped and turned back to watch Melvin disappear over the rise toward his house.   "Driving a tractor doesn't make you all grownup, Johnny."

"I know that, cripes, I know that, but I'm as old as Melvin, ya know, and look at all the stuff he knows."

"He doesn't know anything," Will said and turned once more toward the house.

"Ya?   Like what doesn't he know?" I persisted, running out in front of my cousin and facing him.

Will stopped and waved toward the house.   I turned and saw my mother waving back and I knew everything was O.K. at the house.

"All right.   You think you can fill those britches. Let's see if you can put it all together, big shot."   He turned off along the fence line toward the barns.

~ ~ ~ ~

I often wonder where other people got their lessons, who their mentors were, and whether it was as difficult for them as it seemed to be for me.   I wonder, too, if I have been anybody's mentor and whether I have been as good at it as Will was.   We walked up the hill past the milking barn and over to the tractor shed.   Will was walking fast like he had made up his mind and was determined to get us past the ugliness Melvin had put in our way before the storm.   When we stopped by the big John Deere resting in the shade, I just naturally jumped up on the seat and ran my fingers over the worn black steering wheel.

~ ~ ~ ~

"You love that tractor don't ya?"

"Ya," I said with my usual big smile whenever I thought about driving it.   "She's really somthin', isn't she?   Uncle Shay says they don't make 'em like this 'ol girl anymore."   I jumped off and ran my hand along the big tire.   "Look at the size of these, Will.   I bet she could go anywhere in the whole world."

"You like to touch her, don't you?"   I was surprised at how softly he said it and in such a strange tone.

"Ya.   She's cool and you can feel all that power just waiting for you."

"If you love her what would you do for her?"

This was getting serious and if it was going to be anything like the rest of my summer, I suspected I was going to miss the point.

"What da ya mean?   What would I do for her?"

"I mean would ya die for her or give up baseball for her or what?"

"Cripes, its just a tractor, Will."

"Then you don't really love her, do ya?"   He turned and walked out of the shed and said over his shoulder, "And quit sayin' 'cripes' and 'jeeze' all the time. You sound like a three-year-old."

Running after him and hoping to get the subject back on track, I said, "So what's that got to do with Hobson and all?"

I almost bumped into him as he turned to face me.

"How about your cousin, Vanessa? Do you love her?" He challenged.

"Ya, course I do. Why?"

"You love her so much you'd give up something for her?"

"Well, ya I guess. Sure I would. Cripes....what the hel...jeeze"

"Hey, Essie, come on over here a sec." He yelled across the yard to my cousin.

When she was at our side, I stood watching Will, not having any idea what this was all about and once again sorry I had asked.

"Essie, give your cousin a big hug and plant a big wet one on him. He says he loves you like crazy."

Vanessa was more than willing to go along with the game and came at me with her lips puckered and arms outstretched.

"Jeeze, Essie," I moaned, "I didn't mean I wanted ya slobbering all over me."

"So ya don't know nothin', do ya big shot?" And he walked off toward the corn crib.

We sat for a long time on top of the crib and looked out toward the road where we could see the men coming back from the field. I was confused and afraid to ask any more questions for fear of getting some grownup double talk I couldn't understand. Will was chewing on a weed like a contented cow.

"So..try this, Johnny. Take how ya feel about the Johnny Popper, put that together with how you feel about Essie, and then think about how you feel when you think about Lynn Galvin."

"Lynn Galvin? What about Lynn Galvin?"

"I saw you two down by the lake."

"We were swimmin'. We didn't do nothin'!" I was so nervous I was afraid my voice would crack.

"So put all that together and think about what Hobson said."

In later years, I got somewhat better at assimilating ideas, but on that afternoon it took me a very long time. Will was patient. He just stared out across the sky watching the clouds roll toward another place, another farm, and I dug my toe into the wooden slats of the roof and really tried to "ponder." I thought mostly of the girl who had shone like a golden goddess above the water and about my hands running along the polished flywheel of the John Deere and Hobson and....

"Shit, Will." It came out very softly from my heaving chest.

Will laughed out loud and put his arm around my shoulder.

"Ya, Cousin. Shit is right."

"But that's not what Hobson was saying."

"Sounds the same, doesn't it?"

"Ya, but it doesn't....feel the same."

"No, it sure doesn't."

"You, you mean...," I stammered. "You...I mean Melvin saw.....?"

"That, Mr. Too-Big-For-Your-Britches, is still none of your business."

My admiration for my cousin Will took a giant leap forward that day.

CHAPTER VII

*You must crack the nuts
before you can eat the kernel*

Over the coppery tips of the cornfield, the brown hills rolled up in silence against the horizon. A dust cloud moved ponderously across the whitened blue sky all but obscuring the tiny green speck of a tractor at its center. A weathered gray hay shed leaned into the corner of Barnaby Shea's vision adding to his desolate mood. Barney Shea dropped one hip against the old Packard, as if for support, and sighed a great sigh. Down a small dip in the road and around the bend less than a half a mile was his destination. He had only to return to the sunbaked car, turn the key, and continue on. He would arrive in a matter of minutes. Yet, he had been standing there for over an hour hardly noticing the hot sand and gravel burning through his thin, leather soled shoes. It would take a supreme act of will to go on. He knew he must and still he stood, as empty of the desire to move as the land he stood upon.

In rural America, in fact, in small communities everywhere I suspect, there is nothing loved quite so much as a good secret and even though everyone knows the secret, or at least their own version of it, the thrilling tickle of it vibrates through the people in a way unique to small town life.   There was, I remember, no secret loved as much and, consequently, known as well as the history and inner heart of Barney Shea.   Even as children, or perhaps even more because we were children, we knew the secret best.   Some of it we invented to please our fantasies, some of it we heard from children's shadows, those places where children stand and adults simply do not see.   But most of it we knew because, as Melvin Hobson always said, "If a flea farts in Kilkerry you can smell it all the way to the crossroads." And so it was that when Father Barnaby Shea came to Kilkerry in August of 1949 there wasn't much of his story we didn't already know.   When he first arrived I was only seven years old.   He heard my confession every Saturday afternoon, gave me my first communion, was there for my confirmation, and buried everyone who died in St. Canice parish for almost forty years.   Later, much later, when we all truly knew as much about Barney Shea's business as we did about everyone else's, it was confirmed that, in the beginning, he was not pleased with his assignment.   He was not pleased with his Bishop and, even more, he was not pleased with himself.   The Bishop knew him, had played chess with him every afternoon for years. While contemplating their moves, which were really less important than the rest, they discussed the world's events, the complexity of the church, and great books. They had shared the symphony together and evenings at the theatre. They were friends, adversaries on occasion, but always friends. He tried not to be displeased with the Bishop. The Bishop, he thought, must see the reason for sending him here. What truly angered him was that he could not see it himself. How could God have a plan for him, Barnaby Shea, in a place so devoid of anything familiar to him? What was it, he wondered, God thought he could offer to a world so lacking in the quality of life he was accustomed to? The cornfields gave no answer. Barnaby Shea sighed again, not for the last time, and said aloud, "Thy will be done." Then he mumbled as he opened the car door, "Dammit to hell, anyway."

He had been prepared for the small town itself. They were, after all, the same the world over, towns that had once sprung into existence to serve the needs of a rural community. Gradually, as greater distances could be traveled in a shorter time, the larger cities grew larger and the small towns sat patiently still as if waiting for another time, knowing certainly that it would never come.

He was not surprised, either, by the single dusty street that was the main thoroughfare nor by the raised boardwalk that fronted Farley's General Store, the drug store and fountain, Doctor Orper's office, and two or three empty buildings. Across the street was the old newspaper office now an annex for the local vet. On the other corner was the old blacksmith shop that was now Perley Kin's Garage. On the two side streets to the east and the west and around the block were scattered the few small houses left in Kilkerry, all with the standard picket fence in terrible disrepair. This, he moaned, was his parish. Later he would discover that we came from many miles to attend St. Canice and that he was to shepherd a flock much larger than he anticipated.

He was also prepared for the church. There had been no false hopes, no illusions, about what he would find in that respect. He recalled his Bishop's words quite clearly.

"You will take this little wooden church, Barnaby, with its small congregation and its even smaller income and you will care for, nurture, and love both the church and your parishioners because this is where God intends you to be. This is where I intend you to be. And now let us eat. Our supper is getting cold."

The Bishop had been firm. Father Shea had been depressed. So the small white church with its single bell tower that was almost hidden by the surrounding trees was no surprise. The church, the schoolhouse, and the rectory made up the block just north of the town. Many would have called the picture of those white buildings topped with green roofs and placed in the middle of the well-tended lawns, surrounded by ancient trees for perfect shade nothing short of charming, pastoral, or bucolic. Father Shea longed for a scotch, a room filled with Mozart, and a new Bishop.

If Father Shea was worried about how he would

fit into the small community, the parishioners were equally worried. They had been sent any number of priests to serve the parish. Priests who couldn't fit in anywhere else and were sent "out of the way." Priests too young and priests too old, but mostly priests who wanted only to be somewhere else. On our way to church that first Sunday after Father Shea's arrival, I remember the whole family speculating on "How long this one would last" and "Why didn't the Bishop have the good sense to send them a priest who wanted to be here?"

All that week before, Father Shea had been getting ready. He had been writing his first sermon, organizing the small picnic that would take place on the lawn following the last Mass, going over and over in his head what he would say to "these people" and generally preparing himself to meet his congregation.

The Gospel for that coming Sunday was taken from Mark and it contained the parable of The Sower. The same parable appeared in Matthew and Luke but he liked Mark's version the best. He thought this would be a fine opportunity to introduce to his new congregation some of the similarities and differences in the Gospels, challenge them to break down some of the old barriers and find the truth of the Scriptures. He thought he would have coffee and perhaps some punch and a few sweets outside on the lawn, which would provide the parishioners a chance to meet him and he, in turn, could tell them of his plans. By Sunday morning he was in high spirits. The scotch he had had with breakfast got him through the early Mass and one taken just before the altar boys arrived for late Mass had calmed him once again. He had brought some of his own vestments with him. As the small bell was rung in the sacristy to announce his entrance, he smoothed the fine material of his vestment knowing the love his sister had sewn into it, gripped the golden chalice tightly, and followed the altar boys with a kind of trumped up confidence.

He was vaguely aware of the organ being played by Sister Thomas Marie, the young nun who had arrived only weeks before him and who would be teaching grades six through eight in the fall. He felt the warmth of the sun as it streamed through narrow stained glass windows above him. He saw the people before him and heard them kneel and stand and watched them line up to receive communion at the polished wooden rail that kept them at a distance. He heard himself raise his voice in the pulpit, saw himself raise his arm and point toward the unfamiliar faces. Yet, he moved through it all without any real sensation. He thought of how it felt when he dove into the pool at the seminary. All the sounds coming from a long way off, muffled and unclear as he glided through the water.

He stumbled, caught himself on the cabinet in the sacristy and fought to get air into his lungs. One of the altar boys reached out to him and asked if he was all right.

"Yes, yes I'm fine, just a little dizzy. The heat I think. You boys be careful when you hang up those surpluses, now, we don't want to have to iron them again."

With an effort he began to remove his vestments

and sent the boys on ahead to help Sister with the refreshments. He knew it had not gone well. He did not want to go outside. First he would have a good two fingers, no, four fingers of scotch and then he would slip back to the rectory after everyone had left. First the scotch.

He was about to reach for the bottle secreted away in a bottom drawer when he heard the soft steps and the rattle of her long wooden rosary.

"Yes, Sister, what is it?" he said without turning.

"I'm sorry to intrude, Father. One of the boys said you were not feeling well. I was only wondering...."

Her voice would remain clear in his memory long after she was gone. It was soft, but not monotonous. It was the same voice that kept our attention in class, coached us through our first baseball season to ignominious defeat, and that healed many a broken heart. If she were aware of her effect on others, she gave no sign of it. We all knew she was a saint. We had canonized her long before she left us. She touched the heart of Father Shea that Sunday morning and the sheer danger of it provoked his anger.

"You need not play nursemaid, Sister. I'm fine. I'll be joining you in a moment. Thank you, all the same."

Sister Thomas Marie was not fooled by his brusqueness; none of us were. He was under the impression that the sharpness of his tongue, given edge by his wit, gave him a reputation as the terror of Kilkerry. Actually, everyone saw through it from the very first day and loved him all the more for the way he played the game.

"We're all a little afraid, Father. Perhaps you should take a little fortification before facing the angry masses outside your door." With this and a polite smile she turned with a swish of her skirts and was gone.

"Dammit to hell!" he muttered. "Angry masses. Damn busybody nuns are all alike. God save me from nuns and Bishops who think they know God's will. God save you period, Barnaby." This last was said to a mirror as he downed his Scotch in one gulp and turned for the door.

None of us were being quite as hard on the new priest as he was on himself. There were some questioning looks exchanged and a few wondering nods of the head. But to the parishioners of St. Canice, this was their new shepherd, their parish priest. They would accept him first, welcome him, and then, in good time, change him. I heard my grandfather say, "You'd think they were sending us horses, the way we have to break them in." Yet, when Father Shea stepped out of the front doors and onto the steps of his new church, he knew he had made a terrible mistake. The applause was generous and the faces filled with welcoming smiles. But a cold draft swept down the aisle of the church and out the door. It gripped the young priest in the small of his back. Perhaps it was that moment he was thinking of when he told me some years later, "There are times, Johnny, when no amount of assurances, no logical arguments, will sway you from what you feel at the base of your spine."

Father Barnaby Shea knew that he had failed on his first Sunday at St. Canice. He knew that he had misjudged the people. As he walked through the small gathering and shook hands and said inane things to questions or comments he didn't hear, he tried to understand what it was that he had done or not done. In what way had he so completely botched it? What was it that hid just below the surface in the faces, in the clasp of the hands, in the solicitous voices? He knew he was not mistaken. He had wronged these people and he didn't know how. He did know that if it took the rest of his life, he would find out and he would make it right.

The following weeks were filled with both reward and frustration for Father Shea. He met with the altar boys, he met with the Knights of Columbus, and he met with the ladies of the Altar and Rosary Society. He made it through the latter only because he had also met Thomas O'Grady, who let it be known in a whisper that, "He could get his hands on a bit of Poteen and, if the Good Father wouldn't be offended, they might share a drop or two. Just to clear the dust away, of course." The illegal brew set both Father Shea's stomach and his courage on fire and solidified a friendship that lasted longer than either of them could finally remember.

Father Shea also visited the sick, made arrangements for repairs on the school building and purchased a new stove for the rectory kitchen, and baptized Clara Hobson's first baby. Masses were well attended and there were always nice comments about the sermons.   Still, the new pastor knew he was missing something.   He felt that if he could put his finger on it, he would have the key to being successful in his new assignment.   The feeling gnawed away at his confidence and undermined any sense of success. I like to think, because I played a small part in it, that there was a turning point for Father Shea that summer. I, at least, saw a change in him and it made me happy to watch him grow more comfortable.

This educated and cultured man loved music. His small rooms at the rectory were always filled with sounds of great composers and when the record player or the radio was not available, he heard the great melodies in his head.   He missed not having music in his church.   Oh, there was Sister Thomas and the organ and the lady who came from Montgomery to sing for funerals and weddings.   But he longed for voices raised in prayer.   It was, he thought, the highest form of prayer.   He wanted to hear the Ava Maria, The Lord's Prayer, and others.   He couldn't imagine the month of May without Mother Mary, or the Lenten season without the Tantum Ergo.   It was difficult to find adults who had the time, although later he accomplished that too.   To begin with, though, he found his answer in a children's choir.

We were a small group to start with.   The girls outnumbered the boys three to one.   But after our debut late in July, our numbers grew.   Word got out that it wasn't just singing on Sunday and rehearsals twice a week.   There were also rumors of picnics and trips to Excelsior Park that included, among other things, a monster roller coaster.   Eventually we were all there on Tuesday and Thursday evenings for rehearsals. Melvin was our only bass and never tired of telling us we were all eunuchs, which meant, he explained, that we all "had our nuts cut off at birth and would talk and sing in high pitched voices all our lives." How then, we wanted to know, did he explain that we obviously had our nuts since they were plain to see?

"Because," he said, "they sew peach pits into the sacks so that the only way you can tell if you've got real nuts and not peach pits is if you can sing bass."

My sister was in the choir, too, and several of my cousins and Lynn and Richard Galvin. Lynn and I stood together because she sang soprano and I sang first tenor. She would pretend to be concentrating real hard, looking right at Father Shea and Sister Thomas and all the time she would be rubbing some part of her body against some part of mine. I was scared to death that she would discover I had peach pits instead of nuts, but I wouldn't have moved from that spot for anything. Tuesday and Thursday nights became the highlight of my week.

For Father Barnaby Shea, too, those evenings took on a very special meaning. He would stand next to Sister Thomas as he directed and then, when there was something to be talked over, a harmony changed or a tempo altered, he would slide next to her on the organ bench and they would smile and touch. Nobody noticed but me I'm sure, but then, I was having a parallel experience. It may have been only that they sensed each other's loneliness. As a boy I thought only that they had become fast friends. As an adult I suspect that if their bodies had not touched with intimacy certainly their hearts had. Added to the joy of being near Sister Thomas, Father Shea was also able to bring music into his church.

"I want the sound of your voices to fill this church," he would say, "Let the music touch each corner from the vestibule to the top of the bell tower. The pews may be filled, indeed, but there is always more room for music."

And we would sing because we saw how happy it made him, and our parents and friends said we sounded like the Vienna Boys Choir and I got to stand next to Lynn and Melvin's virility was reinforced. Mondays, however, were always a let down for Father Shea. It was the most difficult day of the week for him and it took just a bit more time with Thomas O'Grady to get through his post Sunday depression. On one such Monday, after having spent the better part of the morning in the back of Perley Kin's Garage with Thomas, he sat on his back porch, the melancholy notes of Rachmaninoff drifting out to the backyard where Sister Thomas and Sister Marian James were hanging out the laundry. When Sister Thomas turned and smiled, he wondered, vaguely, why he was never embarrassed that she handled his underwear. In most parishes they could afford to hire a housekeeper to do those things and she would invariably be one hundred and eight years old. When the two nuns had emptied the basket and Sister Marian James had returned to the small house that served as a convent, the younger sister walked to the edge of the porch steps.

"A melancholy Monday, Father? And the sun so

bright? And the afternoon just barely beginning?"

"If you want to be cheerful, go do it on somebody else's porch, Sister.   This one is reserved for melancholy failures and their kindred spirits."

"Oh, I see. You won't be cheered then, or offer a tired charwoman a cold glass of lemonade?" Her voice was so gentle, he thought, like notes from a harpsichord beneath a virtuoso's hands.

"Oh, well sit if you must and I'll get you something. But none of this cheery talk. I want to talk about storm clouds and doom."

When he returned she was sitting on the top step her long skirt tucked under the toes of her shoes. She was hugging her knees like a small girl. She was a long way from the chair he sat in.

"As long as we are going to talk about doom, Father, let's talk about you." He gave her a startled look, but she wasn't looking at him. "I want to scold you, Father. I want to scold you for thinking that all of your education and upbringing places you above those you were sent to serve." He started to protest but she waved him silent.   "It isn't your job to broaden the hearts and minds of your parishioners. It is your job to broaden yourself instead." She turned to him then and there was just a trace of moisture in her eyes. "Unless you learn to love what they love, fear what they fear, laugh with them and cry with them; unless you learn to do that, Barnaby, you are doomed. Doomed to failed sermons and melancholy Mondays. If you want to touch their souls, then you must learn to enter their hearts."

Barnaby Shea didn't say anything for a long time.

He stood and walked to the railing of his porch and looked across the lawn to the spire of his church. Finally he said, "So, this is the kind of talk I get in return for lemonade and my pleasant company."

"I'm sorry," she said.

"No. Don't be."

The ice cubes melted in the lemonade. The clothes waved gently in the warm summer afternoon and the brown hills rolled up in silence against the horizon.

CHAPTER VIII

A windy day is
not the day for thatching

The room was a mixture of blacks and whites, darkened corners and shadowed silhouettes sleeping in the late afternoon. The sunlight, broken into splotchy patterns by the lilacs outside and the lacy curtain intruded only enough to illuminate the intensity in her eyes and the photo album she held in her lap. Aunt Bridey guided the fingers of her frail hand over the pages as though she were afraid to disturb what rested there. I had fluffed her pillows and drawn her shawl around her shoulders and, at her request, had fetched the old album from a dusty shelf. My other two aunts napped soundlessly in the grayness outside our small pool of light while Aunt Bridey whispered to me about what or who was revealed in the yellowing photos. Her left hand rested on top of mine, jiggling slightly in cadence with the involuntary shake of her head. I could feel the coarseness of her bed covers. She was a mixture of unpleasant odors, of medicine and rancid drool, old powders and soiled gowns. Yet, capped in her white cotton sock, every bit of her fragile energy focused on the memories before her, there was a sweetness about her. I snuggled just a little closer to her on the edge of the bed. She was pleased.

"This was my father, there you see, and I am the smallest one on his right. Oh my, I look frail there, don't I? I wasn't you know, Jackie, I was very hearty and quite a handful, I dare say."

She looked at each picture very carefully sometimes making a comment sometimes simply nodding or sighing or clucking a bit.

"And here, here, this one, Jackie. There is your mother when she was very young."

It wasn't my mother, of course, but my grandmother. I didn't feel it was necessary to correct her. It wasn't as important what we were looking at, I knew, as that we were spending the time together. That is, until she came to one particular picture that was in the center of one page all alone. At this picture her hand stopped. She took her left hand away from mine and placed it very gently on top of the picture like a blind person trying to read the image on the paper.

"And that, Aunt Bridey, who is that?"

"Why that's a picture of..." She moved her fingers to the edge of the picture tracing the outline very delicately. "That is a picture of Mr. McCormick. Mr. Liam McCormick."

When I didn't say anything, she turned to me,

her head not moving, her eyes sparkling.

"Oh, if I could only tell you about Liam McCormick, Jackie, if only I had the strength to tell you, perhaps....."

"Perhaps what, Aunt Bridey?" But her attention was back on the picture.

I came to know Liam McCormick, partly from my aunt and partly from others. I hear the story always in her voice. I see it through her eyes.

~ ~ ~ ~

Liam McCormick laughed too easily. Smoke appeared mysteriously in small explosions from an opening lost to sight beneath the massive growth of brownish red facial hair that spread from just beneath the tanned cheekbone to a full inch under the line of his jaw. Only in more relaxed moments when he laughed deeply from the warmth of his heart did the perfectly white teeth and azure eyes show themselves. On this particular summer evening, one my great aunt remembered in every detail, his eyes had self-consciously settled to gray and restrained themselves from looking directly at her or even from lingering too long on the space surrounding her. He was laughing at something he had just said or something she had said or, perhaps, at nothing. His right hand gripped the baluster of the porch, more for a sense of security than for support, the other hung casually from a thumb stuck into his watch pocket. The sound of his own discomfort diminished over the lawn that sloped down to the road and he fell silent.

Bridget watched him and the flickering glow at the end of his cigar as he puffed and looked off into the evening. She had allowed him this small breach of etiquette since, after all, she was the one who had stolen him away from the other men before he could share the pleasure of male after-dinner cigars and political agricultural philosophizing. The women had, as always, allowed the men to drift out to the back side of the veranda that ran the full length of two sides of the house. They themselves refilled their cups and retired to the parlor to assess the meal, their men, and the poor unfortunates who had no parlor in which to discuss such things. Bridget had watched Mr. McCormick at the dinner table just as she watched him now. She had decided as he, in turn, watched her sister, Margreg, that this evening she would take his arm and lead him outside before either Margreg or the other men could gain their hold on him. The Judge, my great grandfather, had engaged him in every possible topic of conversation beginning shortly after McCormick had arrived and continuing all through dinner. The Judge would measure the young man's responses, raise a suspicious eyebrow or nod with apparent approval, and then move on to the next subject. Margreg had glanced his way more than once and smiled with her usual mixture of reserve and invitation. Bridget knew that if she did not move at exactly the right moment, she would lose him to one or the other.

Now she waited and watched as the meadow smell, full of evening and July, came on a breeze that pushed at his unruly hair and tugged at her hem. She had stood five or six feet away from him, ostensibly to avoid the smoke, but more so that she could use the distance and the growing shadows to study the strangely awkward and gentle man who was so ill at ease in her presence. My Aunt Bridey was the youngest of my three great aunts and it seemed to her that most young men were more interested in her sisters, Margreg and Jane. They treated her as though she were not yet to be taken seriously. But this time, she sensed it was different. Perhaps it was only the lingering warmth of the summer day still holding capture the singular sounds and the sweet, sharp smells of a working farm. Or, perhaps, she was simply becoming aware of herself as a woman. She sensed that this young man, Liam McCormick, was aware of her too and he was uncomfortable. She smiled at the feeling tingling the soft flesh beneath her summer frock. She supposed she might do something to put him at ease. Yet, she was enjoying seeing him as a perspective beau and enjoying, too, the fact that she was putting him on edge. His profile was cleanly etched against the sandy sky and she wanted him to remain there a moment longer.

My aunt was not a fanciful woman. The Judge brooked no flights into dream worlds, worlds that might negate the strength and the purpose upon which rested the Laney name and the future it promised. Beaumont County and, indeed, the great state of Minnesota looked to Judge J. Thomas Laney and Judge J. Thomas Laney looked to his family, especially to his daughters, to reflect only those qualities of breeding and culture that came with the name. Of course, the Judge never reflected on the history of that name and the earth from which it had sprung.   The Judge maintained the farm only as a symbol. Someone else handled the livestock, repaired the buildings, and worked the land. Someone whose name had very much the same ring to it as Laney.

"Oh it was very different in those days, Jackie," my aunt would say, "My, yes, very different."

Bridget was schooled well, not only by the Judge and her mother, but by her sisters as well. Still, she had her fantasies and as the evening surrendered itself to a smattering of stars and a chill on the air, Bridget watched that profile and spun her dreams around all she saw there. His strength, she thought, would take her away from the farm, Kilkerry, Beaumont County and build her a world of friends and conversation that mattered.   His gentleness would protect her and keep her safe.   His youth would be their springboard and they would grow old together but never die. She dreamed all this and more because she felt his touch still upon her hand from his greeting of more than four hours before.   She foresaw all of this because she thrilled remembering the sound of his voice across the dinner table. And she knew it could all come true, because he stood here now and was uneasy because he was aware of her.

Without turning, he inclined his head slightly and cleared his throat.

"Miss Bridget, it's a beautiful evening, for a fact, it is."

Still looking at him and struck again by the deep timbre of his voice, it was a moment before she could answer and suddenly he turned and took a step toward her.

"Or, perhaps, it is only a fair evening like many others, but for the beauty you bring to it."

Bridget caught her breath and the railing with her fingertips as she turned away in a flush. She heard his footsteps behind her, but she dared not look. She stood rigid within herself and waited. The woman in her might have waited for a very long time but after only a moment, the girl swung around boldly to face his approach. He was gone. Only a hint of laughter spilling out of the parlor and a mixture of smoke and politics from around the corner filled the empty space.

~ ~ ~ ~

"I have never been so frightened before or since, Jackie." She told me as she pulled her shawl closer. "Not even now, when I am old and sick. Not even now am I as frightened and lonely as I was when I turned and he was gone."

"You never saw him again then, Aunt Bridey?"

"Oh, yes. Yes, I did see him again. Just once."

~ ~ ~ ~

Liam McCormick returned only once to the Judge's farm after that night. He came up the long stretch of road, a wavering image strangely out of focus in the summer dust and sun. He rode with his back straight but comfortable, one hand fingering the reins and resting on the pommel, the other quiet on the middle of his thigh. He was looking at the house as if, under his gaze, it would bend to his will. Bridget looked up from her needlework and watched as long as she dared, then bolted for her room. She sat rigid at the foot of her bed, the tip of her toe tracing an unconscious pattern in the air, her hands clasped in the folds of her dress, her heart pressing at her throat. She thought back to how, late at night, the comforter thrown off, her nightgown clinging to the curves of her body in the early August heat, she had tried to find the answer to her puzzle. Why had he said those words, spoken them with such strength, so gallant, when only moments before he had seemed so much the awkward youth? And why had he left her then, the palms of her hands cold and damp, her breast warm and lifted? Was he like all the others, teasing the younger sister, the little Bridey they all smiled at sweetly as though she were still a child? How could she have been so naive? To think he might actually be interested in her when there was Jane or Margreg.

She moved from her position on the bed only once to lift the edge of the curtain and watch McCormick give his horse over to the care of young Seamus and approach the front walk, then she retreated to her station. Saturday was a working day. Surely this was not a social call. Yet, if it were business, everyone knew the Judge kept strict office hours in town and would not, under normal circumstances, break that rule. Had McCormick been summoned by the Judge? That, too, seemed unlikely. She had heard that the Judge looked on Liam McCormick's father as an ugly example of the shanty Irish, a different breed altogether from that of his own family.

My own father could remember well the words of this fiercely independent, self-righteous man. "They left their ancestors to be feastin' on black potatoes and sneerin' English while they ran away to build no more of a future than they left behind. They own no land, none of the good Lord's earth. He may be forgivin'' 'em, that's his business sure, but I'll not and I'll be havin' no time for him or any of his kind." Still, since the old McCormick passed away, young Liam had brought respect to the name and many thought him a man to follow.

Holding her breath and fingering the little tufts on the quilt, Bridget listened carefully. She could tell by the sounds that he had been shown to the parlor and not to the Judge's office at the back of the house. She could hear, too, the ring of china and her mother's voice as she made him comfortable. Bridget thought she might go down, but what would she say? What could she say to him? He had left her feeling foolish and empty when only the moment before she had felt so full, a girl so aware of her growing maturity and then suddenly conscious of her vulnerability. Had she, she wondered, been filled by the summer evening and the sense of the moment, or was it Liam McCormick who had quickened her pulse and who caused, even now, the perspiration to wet her palms?

She was startled to hear her name spoken in that same deep resonant voice she had heard when she was introduced to him and then she heard the Judge's footsteps in the hall.

"McCormick, is it? I've been expecting a call from you. No, no, lad, don't get up."

And then the parlor doors slid shut and Bridget let out her breath. The muffled voices continued, heard faintly as they drifted out the windows. In the yard beneath her, a single Rhode Island Red was scratching, pacing to and fro, its head bobbing to its even steps. Below in the meadow, young Seamus had taken cool well water to the working men who drooped for a moment in the shade of the wagons while the two Morgans swished at flies and scraped the meadow floor. God smiled on that quarter section of land that skirted Lake Cullen. He enriched the soil. He fed the cows and fattened the hogs. He lavished His grace on this bit of transplanted Ireland. The Judge had much to be thankful for and to protect for the future. It was his responsibility.

Bridget jerked her head up. The hen fluttered and clucked as the Judge's voice suddenly boomed into the afternoon. The words were indistinguishable, but the tone was the courtroom tone of authority and finality. There was a moment of silence before Bridget heard the doors slide open and the Judge retire to his office. Again Bridget's mother spoke quietly with comfort and reassurance in her voice as always and then the screen door slammed shut and Bridget was alone. She watched McCormick ride down to the road and watched even far into the golden distance of God's smile. She watched him proud and straight until long after he was gone from view.

~ ~ ~ ~

I watched my Great Aunt Bridey rest her shaking hand on the album page. One worn and wrinkled finger, spotted with age, pointed to the man with large, gentle hands and what could have been a reddish beard. Her lips still formed a telling smile and her tired eyes filled with moisture. She was not to know for many years that Liam McCormick had ridden the hill to the Judge's farm that Saturday to ask permission to court young Bridget Laney, "his intentions being strictly honorable and her happiness his solitary goal in life." The Judge had found him unacceptable. His daughter "would not be mixin' with the likes of Patrick McCormick's kin."

And that was his final word for then and always.

CHAPTER IX

*It's no use boiling your
cabbage twice*

I was off by myself trailing a stick along the muddy bank of Cow Creek, kicking whatever was loose under my feet into the murky water. I was cursing under my breath every cuss word I knew and some I had improvised for the first time. With each step, my frustration grew and with it came more senseless anger. I cursed my father and my mother and my stupid sister for agreeing with them and for being my stupid sister in the first place. Every weed or stem or small branch that got in my way fell victim to an angry kick or a swipe of my stick. Lewis had sensed my mood and hadn't even followed me out of the yard. I was alone. I was without friends or family or even a dog who had any sympathy for how I felt or what I wanted. All anybody could talk about was how important it was to make decisions for our future happiness. Big deal, I thought, as I chucked a big dirt clod into the creek. Big Deal! I wasn't concerned about the future. I was concerned about hunting season being just around the corner and the choir picnic next week and getting rubbed against by Lynn Galvin on Thursday night and that was as much of a future as I gave a damn about. And as far as happiness goes, I was perfectly happy with things just the way they were. If my sister would dry up and blow away and if I didn't have to confess my impure thoughts to Father Shea on Saturday, I would be perfectly happy. They were all being so selfish and nobody would listen to me. Why would they want to move to the city when all that was really important was right here? My grandfather said not to worry over much about it, because it wasn't going to happen for awhile if it happened at all and I hated him too, a little bit, because he seemed to be on their side.

In an effort to gain more distance from a world that was not going the way I wanted it to, I had climbed a gnarled old oak that suited my mood perfectly. Wedged comfortably in the arms of this old friend, I could look up to the constant sky or out across Lake Cullen to the steeple of St. Canice and the countryside beyond. I could not see the farm waving in the heat behind me. That was just fine. I did not want to see the farm or think about the people who sat around the kitchen table and made plans for my future. There were other things to think about, other people to dream about. I often came to that old oak tree and climbed into its shady security. It was where I did my best daydreaming. I always felt, and even now I tend to agree, that daydreams are the very best kind of dreams.   They can be shaped any way the dreamer likes and if the dream doesn't work out exactly right, it can be changed at will.   Since nobody else is privy to a person's dreams, nobody can criticize or contradict the choices made or the way in which reality is bent.   At age thirteen I was a specialist, even a virtuoso daydreamer.   On that particular summer afternoon, I was about to shape the future the way I wanted it to be.

I was just about to work in the part where Lynn and I would take over the old store and turn it into a real success when the church spire disappeared from my view for a moment and then reappeared.   I watched for a moment and then it happened again as though a very low cloud....

"Cripes, I mean shit, that's smoke!" I yelled as I scrambled up to the next highest branch to get a better look.   I couldn't see much, just a hazy swirl that didn't quite fit the rest of the sky.   I strained my eyes, squinting against the glare, trying to see if it was a dust devil or the trail of a trap truck going too fast up a back road.   But I knew instinctively it was not.   I had lived in the country too long.   I understood what it meant to have firefighting equipment miles away, manned by volunteers who may or may not be close to that equipment.   I lived on a farm without running water and knew what the fear of fire was.   It was definitely smoke and it was coming directly from the center of town.

Both the daydreams and the anger I had been feeling disappeared as I shinnied down the tree and ran toward the far end of the lake and the county road. I saw my uncle's Chevy speeding toward town, trailing a cloud of dust that hung above the road behind him clear back to the crossroad. I waved and shouted but the driver's concentration was on the road and the church spire that could barely be seen behind the thickening smoke. I was almost to the road when I saw something moving through the dusty fog. It looked like a mirage at first, wavering in the center of the county road. It seemed to glide forward above the ground with no sound or definite shape. I remembered a scene from a movie about Arabs and camels and the shifting sands. The hero had ridden out of the dust storm on his white horse and it took him a very long time to take real shape as he galloped toward the camera. I wanted to get to town, but I couldn't take my eyes off this strange apparition. Suddenly a breeze lifted off the lake and swirled the dust away enough for me to see more clearly. The unmistakable form of Melvin Hobson was hunched over the handlebars of his Columbia Flyer and he was peddling for all he was worth. His baseball cap was turned backwards to facilitate wind resistance and I could hear him huffing and groaning as he strained to turn the single sprocket faster.

"Hobson!" I screamed as he flew past me.

I thought he, too, was going to pass me up and then I saw him slam his pedal back. He braked into a skid and disappeared again into his own dust. Without a word, I was on the handlebars. Melvin gave us a running start, leaped onto the seat, and we were off. We were almost there when I could feel Melvin tiring. We were moving slower and he was puffing and groaning faster and louder.

"Switch!" I yelled.

It was a tricky maneuver, but we had choreographed it a hundred times. Even on the gravel road, we accomplished it with clockwork precision. Melvin slid back on the rack over the rear wheel while continuing to peddle. I steered and made the two-move switch from handlebar to seat. The final transfer to the pedals was the most amazing of all. Once on the seat I had to keep my legs high and out over the front wheel. I watched the pedals until I was sure and then yelled, "Now" as Melvin let go and laid his legs out in a wide V behind me. The trick accomplished, we both let loose a few jubilant yells and sped forward.

By the time we reached the edge of town, it was impossible to tell where the fire was. A thick charcoal cloud started several feet above the ground and rose as high as the rooftops where it turned into puffing black billows ghosting into an invisible sky. Everything was cast in a shadow world that altered shape every few seconds as the smoke paled then darkened then paled again. Every few minutes a splotch of color swam through the smoke as flames fought for air. We could hear the fire bell still clanging and muffled shouts as silhouettes darted here and there. Melvin had gotten off the bike and stood staring into the smoke.

"Christ, Laney," he whispered, "The whole damn town is gone. The whole Goddamned town!"

It wasn't just the excitement of a fire, the kind of ambulance-chasing that all kids seem drawn into.

There were people in that choking fog, our friends and family. The smoke was drifting outward and before we realized it we were choking and rubbing our stinging eyes.

"We gotta go in there, Hobson, toward the fire station. We gotta see if we can help." Without waiting for an answer, I pushed the bike forward and headed into the pall. Hobson jumped on the back and shouted frantic instructions to me as though he could see from behind me better than I could. All the time he was pounding on my back and wailing that the whole town was in flames. We had almost reached the end of the the block and the garage that served as a firehouse when something jumped out of the smoke and hit my front wheel. We recovered our balance then lost it and went end over end landing in a heap on top of the dog that had upset us. I was on top of the dog and Hobson was on top of me. All three of us were a yowling jumble of arms, legs, and paws.

"Get off me, Hobson." I screamed. "Get off me, dammit, I can't breath!"

"I can't!"

"What do you mean, you can't? You're on top, for cripes sake."

"I'm not on top. the bike's on top!"

We got untangled, the dog went yapping into the dark and we staggered about trying to get our bearings. I had just righted the bike when we were knocked off our feet again. A deafening explosion shook the ground and sent us into the dust once more. My ears were ringing, but I could hear Melvin screaming. "Jesus God! Jesus God! We're dead. Oh, my God!"

I was spitting out smoke and dirt and rubbing my eyes trying to see what had happened when Hobson jumped on top of me and started choking me with both hands at my neck. He was screaming at me with stinking breath.   "You son of a bitch, Laney. Everywhere I go with you, disaster strikes. You're a fuckin' jinx.   You've really done it now, you son of a bitch!"

Just when I thought he would throttle the life out of me, a pair of able hands grabbed us both by the scruff of the neck and pulled us from the ground. I could hardly breathe and it was difficult to keep my eyes open, but I could plainly see the white dickey of Sister Thomas's habit and hear the sound of the long rosary that hung from her waist as she wrestled us apart.

"Stop this, boys!   Stop it right now!   Melvin Hobson," she shouted, "if your mouth weren't so full of dirt, I would wash it out with soap right here. Now the two of you stop it. We have to get out of this smoke. Now march! No more tomfoolery, just march."

We stumbled on ahead of her as she swished at our butts with the back of her hand. By the time she herded us to the back of the schoolhouse, the smoke had cleared considerably.   What slight breeze there was kept the smoke drifting in another direction. We collapsed on the cool grass, gasping for breath. Sister sat next to us trying to clear her eyes with her hanky while she glared at her two troublesome boys.

"What the hell is burning?" Hobson coughed. He was kneeling on the grass like he was facing Mecca or something, rocking back and forth on his hands and knees.

"Melvin." Sister warned.

"I mean...what's burning, Sister? How bad is it? Laney hit a godda...hit a dog before we could get to the fire station."

That was the last thing I heard as I sank back onto the grass and gathered in the peaceful dream that waited just on the edge of the darkness.

~ ~ ~ ~

I was standing with my father on the top of the hill behind the house. His arm was draped over my shoulder and he was pointing out over the rooftops to the end of the sky. A trail of smoke from the pipe clenched in his teeth curled up and made a little bubble above his head like you see in comic books when people speak. I waited for something to appear in the bubble but it remained empty and then drifted away. Lewis came and sat next to me and I could feel his cold nose on my hand. When I looked down there was a bubble above his head, too, but it was empty as well. My father started to walk down the hill and when I started to follow he shook his head, smiled and waved to me, and then he was gone.

I took Lewis by the hand but it was Lynn and she was pulling me toward the lake. We floated above the ground with Lewis bounding along below us until we reached the shore. When I spoke to Lynn to ask her some very important questions, little empty bubbles came out of my mouth and rose above my head and Lynn smiled like she knew what I was saying then she swung out over the lake on a long rope and disappeared into the sky.   I was running with Lewis, then, through the rows of corn and across the pasture and up and down the creek and we laughed and laughed and then I heard my mother call me and we ran and ran and I could see her waving like she had on the day of the storm.   She called once more and then I couldn't see her anymore and Lewis ran out ahead of me farther and farther until he was just a black speck on top of the hill and I yelled and yelled coughing little empty bubbles out of my mouth.   There were so many bubbles I was beginning to choke.   I dropped to my knees coughing and sputtering…..

~ ~ ~ ~

Father Shea was trying hard to get me to drink the water and Sister Thomas kept dabbing at my forehead with a wet cloth.   "A little too much smoke, young man."   Father Shea was saying, "But you'll be just fine.   Just drink this down, it'll help clear the cobwebs out of your head."

Hobson came charging up, all of his earlier animosity forgotten.

"Hey, Laney Faney, you missed all the excitement.   Come on.   Your dad's gonna take us in the truck down to Kin's Garage, or what's left of it. That's where the fire and the explosion came from. Come on, your dad's waitin'."

When he took a closer look at me he got a little concerned.   Probably thinking he might have done some real damage when he throttled me.   "Hey, is he all right, Father? He doesn't look real good."

"I think he'll be fine, Hobson.   Why don't you give him a hand until he gets his legs back."

Main street was ankle deep in mud. Water had been showered on all of the buildings for hours in an attempt to keep the fire from spreading. The smell of wet wood, smoke, and burned timber assailed my nostrils and made me sneeze. Charred pieces of buildings still smoldered in the mud and ashes around Perley Kin's Garage.

As we made our way to the sudden rubble that used to be the garage, my father explained that a small fire toward the back of the building had caught hold in a pile of old tires which accounted for all the black smoke and the acrid smell that rose above all of the other odors. I was just about to ask about the explosion when I saw the twisted mass of tubing and tanks that had once been Perley Kin's pride and joy. He had spent a good deal more time fussing and clucking around that old apparatus than he had working in his garage. The old timers and some of the younger ones, too, would be burying their heads in their hands and mourning the loss of the only still left in the county. My father had placed one arm around my shoulder and the other around Melvin's as we stood before the melted shrine.

"Not much more than smoke damage to the rest of the town, boys, and the garage can be rebuilt. You can bet your bottom dollar, though, that there was no insurance on this little treasure."

Perley and a few of his cronies were milling around the little circle where only yesterday, they had sat on nail kegs and tires and well worn benches chuckling at old stories retold for the hundredth time. Now the toes of their shoes kicked sadly at the ashes covering the very spot that marked their favorite place to pass a little time, chew a plug, smoke a bowl, or just whittle away a few hours listening to the gurgling and hissing that promised "a drop or two" to slake their thirst.   As I watched those men, hands thrust deep into their overalls, I had some sense that the loss here was not simply a tired old building or even an illegal distillery. Most of us discover some routine in life.   We walk paths that we have come to know and even take for granted.   We can travel them without seeing them, without actually feeling them beneath our feet.   We simply know they are there, a part of the inner sense of who and what we are.

The loss here had more to do with the way in which a particular kind of life was lived, day in and day out, year in and year out.   Certainly there would be new places to gather and even a new still, but they would have little to do with what once was.   I remember pulling closer to my father as I watched Perley dig about in the black mud looking for remnants of what he could never rebuild.   I thought I knew something of what he felt.   I could no longer dredge up any anger about moving, just a kind of wistful chill.

Melvin and I walked through town and picked up his bike.   We extricated it from the mud and debris, kicked at it a bit, straightened the handlebars as best we could and pushed it to the dry edge of town. Except for Melvin's grumbling about the front wheel being bent and how I had really done it this time, we didn't have much to say as we wobbled into the late evening.   He dropped me at the crossroads with a quick "I'll see ya tomorrow," tightened his backward cap on his head and rode off. I watched him for a while as he pedaled into the smoky orange haze looking like a bear on a circus bike. Melvin Hobson had been a part of a path I had walked and I wondered if I would miss him. I turned and started up the road toward the farm when the old REO came bouncing up behind me. I jumped on the running board and leaned in the window, smelling my father's pipe and drinking in his smile as we headed for home.

CHAPTER X

*Men learn the hard way
when they learn at all*

I had been pursued for months by some unknown, unnamed thing. I couldn't call it a definite feeling. It was only a vague sensation of something stalking behind me, propelling me forward compelling me to constantly look surreptitiously over my shoulder in the hope of catching a glimpse of what I only suspected was there. I felt its presence like the imagined dangers that lurk in the dark of night just out of sight and hearing. At the time, I would have been unable to put together all that accounted for this strange, unfathomable sensation. I know now, of course, that I was looking in the wrong direction. It wasn't anything behind me that gave me a feeling of dread. It was, instead, what lay ahead of me.

When I was in college, a group of us had found a place of escape from our studies, and, I suppose, from a world of rules and regulations. It was a secluded spot on the river not frequented by other picnickers or boaters because of the high cliffs that walled in the water at that particular point. It was a quiet, secluded spot, more a narrow lake than a river. It provided us with the opportunity to stand back from the edge, run full tilt for several yards, then fling ourselves over the precipice with shrieks of fear and delight. What I remember most clearly is that instant just after leaving solid ground, that incredible paradox of feeling both exhilarated and panicked all at the same time. That first moment of complete loneliness, loneliness because you have been separated from everything you know to be secure and safe.

It was that moment of loneliness and separation that the events of that summer were pushing me toward. Though I didn't understand what was happening, I knew instinctively what that moment would feel like. I had no way of knowing that it could be exciting and that it would pass into a new kind of security.

In an effort to ease my discomfort, I spent my summer trying to find something exciting, something wonderful. As much as I loved to dream, I wanted a real experience, a fantasy-come-true that would blot out my pursuer. By the middle of August I was panicked. Time was running out. So I was in this desperate state the night we visited the graveyard.

It was Thursday night and we were sweating in the close confines of the choir loft. It was impossible not to fidget, giggle, poke and jab, and otherwise be obnoxious and disruptive. Finally the patience of both Father Shea and Sister Thomas gave way and they suggested we take a break for some fresh air and something to drink. The stampede that followed was typical and I held back for a few minutes to avoid Hobson or, even worse, Wally Bacon either of whom delighted in crushing me against the wall or flinging me down the stairs. Before I could follow in the wake of screams and shouts, Lynn grabbed my hand and pulled me to the other side of the loft and pushed me through the small door that led to the belfry staircase.

"Come on," she whispered, "I'll show you something."

When she eased the door shut so nobody would hear and leaned her back against it, I blurted out, "Well, where is it? What've you got?"

"Shh!" Without saying more she started up the stairs. When I didn't follow, she stopped and looked at me.

"We're not supposed to be up there, Lynn. I mean, what if they catch us?" She just looked down at me and even though I couldn't see her face clearly in the darkness, I could tell she was disgusted.

"Jeeze, Laney," she hissed, "are you always gonna be this dumb? I can't show it to you here. It's too dark and nobody's gonna catch us. Come on."

Suddenly the possibilities began to dawn on me and I started up the stairs after her in such a hurry that I tripped on the first step falling face first into a hundred years accumulation of mouse turds.

"Shh! Be quiet! Or do you wanna forget it?"

"No," I stammered as I picked the filth out of my mouth. "I'm coming. Just wait, will ya?"

We had to climb a small ladder to reach the tiny

room that once held the bell. When I stuck my head through the hatch, Lynn was already sitting with her back to the wall. The moonlight found its way through the louvered slats illuminating her in a silver glow. The dust particles we had disturbed shimmered about her hair and face like fairy dust. I had enough sense to stifle the moan that wanted to escape from my throat, but I couldn't stop the sweat from trickling down my sides nor the trembling in my body.

She just looked at me and smiled, the joy of her secret dancing in her eyes. I sat in front of her and crossed my legs, hands stuffed in the bend at my knees so she wouldn't see them shake.

"I love it up here, don't you?" she whispered. "In the moonlight and all? It's so peaceful and....private."

"Have you been up here lots?" I asked not wanting to hear her say yes.

"A few times. To sit in the moonlight and think and be by myself."

I couldn't help smiling and I scooted a little closer. If she came here by herself, then I was special. I wanted to be cool. I didn't want my anticipation to be obvious, but it was no use.

"What did you want to..to show me, Lynn? I mean, they'll be back for rehearsal soon and.."

"Do you like me, Jackie?" She looked directly at me and I knew even if I told her no, or tried to be casual about it, she would see the truth.

"Yes, I like you. I like you a lot."

"I like you, too." My heart thundered in my chest. I wanted to explain if I could. "Remember by the lake when we went swimming?" But I faltered and couldn't say anymore.

"I remember," she said finally.   "And I kind of promised you...so that's why I wanted to show you..." She looked at me for a long time as if she were trying to read in my face whether she could trust me or not. "You'd better close your eyes, then," she said as she reached across and touched my eyes to make sure I wasn't cheating. I heard her rustling about and held my breath until I couldn't hold it any longer. When I opened my eyes she was holding a velvet case on her lap looking at it as though she were about to cry. She slid from it the pieces of a silver flute, put it together very carefully, and held it out for me to touch.

It shone in the moonlight like white gold.   Her fingertips balanced it so that it seemed to float like magic in the dusty air. When I reached to take it from her, she drew back just a little, hesitated, and then placed it in the open palms of my hands. I closed my hands around the instrument knowing that I had just been presented with a precious gift.   Even so, I felt disappointed, cheated.   I felt, once again, that something had slipped past me.   I would not have dared say, even to myself, that I wanted to see her, touch her, not her old flute, but that is exactly what I felt.   Filled with impotent anger, I handed the flute back to her, rose to my feet, and said over my shoulder as I went for the trap door, "We'd better get back. Oh, and uh..thanks, your flute's real cool."

When the others clamored back up to the loft, it was pretty obvious that something had happened. It was clear what Melvin thought by the leer slashed across his face. Lynn's eyes were red and she hadn't bothered to brush off the dirt from her clothes. Her brother, Richard, kept looking around nervously, first at Lynn and then at me. I tried to look at Sister Thomas with an innocence I didn't feel. I felt as conspicuous as if I had just farted in church during the offertory. I was never so glad to see practice come to an end. My plan to escape into the night as soon as we filed out was foiled by Wally and a few of the others who held me back.

"Hey, Laney, where ya goin'? What's the big hurry?"

"I gotta get home. I told my folks..."

Wally grabbed me in a headlock and gave me a knuckle rub as he pushed me forward. "Naw. We got out early and besides tonight," he raised his voice and tilted his head back as he shouted to the moon, "tonight, we see the widow's ghost." Everybody started to yell and howl like dogs as they shivered and shook in mock fear. I had forgotten that we had planned to visit the graveyard after practice.

There were two graveyards in Kilkerry. One was on a small rise just out of town. The other was several miles away. There had been a church next to the second one as well, but that was long before our time. It was this one that held the legend of the widow's ghost and any number of other ghost stories so, naturally, that was where we all wanted to go. Richard said it was the perfect night because of the bright moon and because it was on this night fifty years ago that the widow's ghost had first been seen. As we zigzagged our way down the road and across the fields, Richard decided to enlighten us all on the history of the Widow Lavern. I kept looking over my shoulder for Lynn, but she wasn't behind us. I had no idea what to say to her, but I knew I had to say something. I had acted like a real schmuck and now, too late, I was sorry and embarrassed.

By the time we reached the wrought iron gates that barred the road into the cemetery, the moon, cold and silent, swam in and out of a few dark clouds. The night was warm, but the shadows beyond the gates gave me goose bumps. The Heffler twins had already headed for home, covering their fear with a simple, "We gotta get going. It's late." My sister and my cousin Will had also turned off at the crossroad and now there was just Melvin and Richard and Wally and me.

The wrought iron actually only ran a few yards to either side where it was replaced by a low stone wall pocked and crumbling like an old battlement. We had started to climb over when Melvin pulled back.

"Christ, I'm not goin' in there with Laney. He's a jinx. Sompin' weird'll happen with him around. Dead bodies 'ill come poppin' out of their graves or some shit like zombies after our souls or some shit."

"Come on, you chicken liver," taunted Wally.

The four of us climbed over the wall and stared into the night. By day the cemetery was one of the most beautiful spots for miles around. The two sides leading away from the road were lined with shade trees that had been there as long as the oldest graves they sheltered. The fourth side was hemmed with just a low hedge of blackberry, leaving a view down the slope and out across the peaceful landscape beyond.

At night, however, with the branches and the clouds shaping and reshaping shadows across the markers of the dead it was enough to give real credence to stories like the widow's ghost. You could almost feel her pushing away the soil packed down upon her body, nails clawing at the dirt her lover had shoveled over her while she was still alive and screaming for his mercy, and finally, as she spat for one last breath, damning his evil soul.

"Well, what do we do now?" Melvin asked. "None of the squeamy, chicken shit girls are left so who the hell we gonna scare?"

"Ya. Hey what happened to your sister, Richard?" Wally asked as he took a few steps forward testing his courage.

"I don't know." He turned to look at me. "What did happen to my sister, Laney?"

"I don't know. I mean, how should I know? I haven't seen her since we left town. I didn't do anything to your sister."

"Ya? That better be right, Laney." He started back over the wall then stopped on the top of it and looked back at me. "That better be right. I'm headin' on in." And the three of us were left alone.

"So, let's take a poke around and see if we can scare anything up?" Melvin laughed a little nervously at his own joke, then he gave me a push. "You go on and lead, Laney Faney. I wanna keep an eye on you."

Wally followed along behind us talking to keep up his pretended courage. "Hey, ya suppose this is really her fiftieth birthday? People say they've heard her up here moaning and wailing for her husband's soul."

"It isn't her birthday, you dip shit." Melvin snapped, "And she doesn't want her husband's soul, she wants her lover's."

"What's the dif?"

"You dipshit!"

We had reached the middle of the cemetery where there was a large shrine of Saint Francis, his moon-washed hand raised out as a perch for a bird just landing, its graceful wings forever lifeless in this place of the dead. Hobson sat down on the pedestal.

"Nobody believes in that shit, anyway. You don't believe in that shit, do ya, Laney?"

Just as he leaned back into the statue, a long low moan drifted out of the ground in front of us and off into the darkness. The crickets stopped as the sound repeated. It would have been difficult to tell the three of us from Saint Francis as we froze in mid-motion. Melvin was the first to move, but he was backing toward the wall.

"What the shit?" The sound of his voice was so reverent the profanity got lost.

"Ah, it's just the wind or somethin'," Wally said as he moved backward with Melvin.

"There ain't no wind, you dipshit!" Melvin hissed.

Just as the low moaning sound died away, there was a shrill wail that shot into the trees and back again. It came from just in front of us as though it were coming from below the surface breaking free in mad exultation. Wally was already over the wall with Melvin not far behind screaming, "I knew it, Laney, you fuckin' jinx." And then the silence returned and I was alone.

I took a few careful steps forward until I could see her shadow beyond the tombstone. I sat down next to her on the damp grass. The moon was blotted out by a cloud and we were in darkness except for a tiny shaft of silver that glimmered on her flute. It was a long, long while before the moon fought clear and washed the tree tops and stretched our shadows out across the graves.

"My grandfather used to make us whistles from the old willow by the creek." I spoke quietly out into the valley, afraid she would get up and leave if I was too abrupt or loud. "He would make them all sizes and some would sound high and clear like the way I whistle for Lewis, and others were low and breathy like my Aunt Mary's voice. They were real neat, but they weren't as special as your flute."

She didn't say anything. She just looked at her flute and finally, without looking at me, she handed it to me by one end. It was as though she didn't care if I took it or not. There was no gift here, no offering of any kind. I took it carefully and held it to my lips. I tried to get some sound, but succeeded only in getting it all wet with spit. I wiped it very carefully then, and held it in my lap. I was afraid she would leave and I had nothing to say to keep her there. Eventually I simply said, "I'm sorry."

"Do you want to see me? Do you want to touch me?"

I was suddenly jerked back to where I had been several hours before, only I wasn't there anymore. I was just sorry. I just wanted her to be here.

"What?" I croaked and turned away. I was really

ashamed that she knew the truth.   She must have known it all along.

"Richard says you just want to see my tits.   He says you don't like me and you don't care about my flute any more than he does. You just want to see my tits."

I couldn't say anything. What could I say? Yes I want to.   No I don't want to.   I didn't know what I wanted anymore.   How could I tell her I wanted to touch her, that I had been dreaming about it all summer?   I mean, it wasn't right that she had asked me.   That was too confusing.   She wasn't suppose to ask me, for Christ's sake!   We were just supposed to do it. I mean, somehow you just did it.   Didn't you?

She had picked up the flute and she played it for a while.   No real tune or melody, just notes mostly, very low and sad like the wind must sound when it blows through the trees when nobody's around to hear it. A song all its own, belonging to the wind itself.

"I like you, Lynn. That's all. I just like you. And the other...well, I don't know, maybe it comes from liking you, maybe it doesn't have anything to do with that.   I don't know.   I know I like you and if you like me, like you said, then that's keen.   That's all then; we just like each other."

She just played some more notes and I felt so miserable I thought my life would end this way, right here in a graveyard.

"It's gittin' late, Lynn, I'd better see you home, huh?"

She put the flute away in the velvet case she must have had hidden in the belfry because it still had little mouse turds all over it, and we stood up to go. When I faced her, the moonlight on her face was broken into little tiny patterns from the leaves on the trees and I remembered how she looked with the fairy dust shimmering around her. We were almost exactly the same height and it was so easy to lean forward and close my eyes. It seemed so natural. That is, after we figured out what to do with the flute and on which side to put our noses. When we finally worked it all out, our lips touched cool and damp in the night air. We moved a little so that our mouths parted some and I could taste her and I could feel her warm breath on my cheek. We held each other like that until we were both dizzy. We let go reluctantly and looked at our feet and moved our hands tentatively.

When we raised our heads and leaned to kiss again, she took my hand and slid it inside her T shirt. I must have done something wrong, because she pulled back slightly and then moved back again against my cupped hand. I didn't move. I just held her and felt her heart beat against my palm and her nipple harden as we kissed.

We held hands as we walked home and kissed again in her front yard while the dogs went nuts and lights came on in the upstairs rooms. I touched her again and she moved against me and touched me once through my jeans, the memory of which drove me crazy for months afterward. She stood with her father on the porch and waved with her flute case in one hand. Mr. Galvin did not look happy, but she did.

When I look back on that night in the graveyard, I remember the wonder of that kiss and the feel of her body next to mine and I realize what a miraculous moment it was. But as I smile remembering it, I am greatly saddened, too, because I realize that the far more intimate moment was in the belfry when she handed me her flute. I had been right at the time. Something had passed me by in my selfishness, an intimacy I would never again recapture.

CHAPTER XI

*When the sky falls
we'll all catch larks*

August was nearly at an end and so, it seemed, was my life on the farm. The sometimes quiet, sometimes heated discussions that had occupied my immediate family since early summer were over. The decision had been made. We were to be moved and settled in by the time school started. It came as a surprise to me that the house had already been purchased and that my sister and I were registered at a school I had never seen. After Labor Day, we would drive to our new home and that would be that.

"Everything will turn out just fine, you'll see," my mother said over and over again whenever she saw the fear or the tears in my eyes. After I became a parent myself, I came to understand that parents live under the delusion that simply making this projection for the future as though they had some kind of parental crystal ball will, in fact, make it so. Even a child knows that everything does not always turn out just fine and anybody who forecasts that it will better have some facts at hand. No matter how many times my mother tried to reassure me, I had my doubts and I was desperately clinging to every thread of my life, past and present. Perhaps I was trying to store things up, things I could take with me.   Like a squirrel gathering nuts for the winter. It seemed my thirst for this gathering could not be satiated. I walked every foot of the farm over and over.   I touched every weathered board, every cracked and knotted fence rail. I clung to the people too, watching them as they moved and talked and worked, listening to them as my father listened to a piano concerto bringing the sound inside, making it a part of himself. I hoarded every sensation as later I would hoard my marbles and my baseball cards.   I gathered and stored and gathered some more only to leave it all behind.   In only a few short months it would be less important than what was happening on any given day. In a few years, it would become only an occasional memory that would make me smile or frown, until many years later when I had the need to gather it all in again, to take the memories out, like an old photo album, and look at the wonder of them.   At the time I didn't understand the need, I just went about storing things up out of fear or love or loneliness.

The most abundant harvest was collected from my great aunts. They were a plethora of information about the farm, its people, and the entire country for miles around. I had once dreaded having to make my daily visit to the "Aunties" room.   It was now something I looked forward to and often, in the last days of August, I would visit them twice a day.   My aunts seemed to enjoy the visits as much as I.   We would have tea and I would make a great ceremony of serving them while they chattered across their beds in the dimness.   They would scold and politely correct each other, insisting that I not be misled or get the wrong idea. It was important to them that the stories they told be accurate.   Often they spent as much time ironing out the details as they did in relating the substance of the story.   If I became impatient, they would lose interest in talking and ask me to return another time when they were less tired.   I learned to listen attentively.   In fact, I came to enjoy their digressions and elaborations most of all and often we would all forget what it was that we had been talking about in the first place.

Sometimes, in a Minnesota August, the heat will pile up for several days not changing more than a few degrees from one morning to the next.   It seems, too, to collect with it, like a cloud gathers moisture, all of the lingering odors both pleasant and malodorous. The result is overpowering.   The days gather around you like a thickening fog, slowing you down and forcing you to take refuge in whatever sliver of shade promises some respite.   On such an afternoon, I had gone to the cellar for cider and brought it with me on my visit to the aunties in the hope of easing their discomfort and mine. However, the glasses grew warm and sticky almost at once.   The stale, fetid air in their room was oppressive, the burden of conversation too much for any of us. So, like four strangers in a hospital waiting room, we fidgeted, cleared our throats, and bore our individual discomforts in silence. The ponderous regularity of the old Seth Thomas seemed to add to the weight I felt crushing down on me so that finally I was about to excuse myself before I suffocated. As I gathered up the glasses, I noticed that Aunt Margreg and Aunt Bridey had fallen asleep. All three of them were so still I might have wandered into the back room of a mortuary except that my Aunt Jane's eyes were following me and she had more than the usual creases across her forehead. She was so intent that I set down the glasses and went to sit on the edge of her bed. When she found the strength to speak I was shocked. I sat there staring at her, but she patted my hand and smiled reassuringly.

"She what?" My Aunt Mary sounded almost frightened when I told her what Aunt Jane had asked. She looked toward my mother with real concern.

"Are you sure that's what she meant, Jackie? There must be some mistake. Your Aunt Jane hasn't been out of her room in years, let alone out of the house."

"She seemed real sure that's what she wanted, Mom, honest. She said, 'Ask Mary to help me dress. I would like to go for a ride'." My mother and Aunt Mary shook their heads at each other and finally Mom said,

"You'd better go check, Mary. If you need help, call me."

Aunt Mary returned still shaking her head, but she was smiling a bit too. "That's what she wants to do. She wants to go for a ride with Jackie. When I asked her where she wanted to go, she actually scolded me, Carol. She said, 'Now, Mary, going for a ride in the afternoon does not mean actually going any place in particular, it simply means going for a ride'."

The thought of my Aunt Mary, at nearly six feet tall, being scolded by the frail little lady in the next room made us all laugh.

"Well, what do we do?" my mother asked the room in general.

There was a long silence with everybody looking at everybody else until finally my Aunt Mary said, "We get her dressed and take her for a ride, I guess. It's just so hot and muggy I...I am worried about her. I don't think she has the strength."

My aunt had a way of sitting at the kitchen table, elbow resting on the table, her face turned into the palm of her hand, her little finger tapping the side of her nose while she thought things through. If she were merely daydreaming, she would hum softly to herself as she tapped her finger. If her thoughts were deliberative, she clicked her tongue against the roof of her mouth until she had come to a conclusion. My mother and I waited patiently because we knew the process could not be rushed. Finally the clicking and the tapping stopped.

"Jackie, would you please go tell your Uncle Shay to bring the Chevy around to the back door?" As I started to leave, my mother called after me. "And fetch the green afghan from the sofa in the front room."

"Mom, its three hundred degrees out there!"

"Just do as you're told," she said as she followed my aunt toward the aunties' room.

By the time they had bathed and dressed Aunt Jane and had quieted the protestations of both Margreg and Bridey, it was late afternoon and the heat was persistent. When Aunt Jane came down the hall and into the kitchen everybody who had been within shouting distance had gathered to witness the event. The adults looked obvious and foolish as they pretended to be there for some other reason, while the kids simply gawked with open astonishment.

She leaned on my uncle's arm using her heavy black cane with the other hand as though it were a dainty parasol. The dress she wore had been retrieved from her youth. It was dandelion yellow with a high, straight collar and a frilly bodice. The skirt hung in limp pleats from her waist almost hiding the incongruous bedroom slippers that held her swollen feet. A sun hat of the same yellow was tilted at an angle on her silver hair with two long yellow ribbons cascading down her back. She looked to me like a small child playing dress-up. Two pink circles of color on her sunken cheeks and a little too much color in her lips that didn't quite follow the natural line of her mouth added to the illusion. But when she smiled and offered her arm to me, she was a beautiful young woman who had slipped through a crack in time. There was a little smattering of applause and a few "Good afternoon Aunt Janes".

She turned to the stunned audience and placed her finger on her lips. "Shh," she cautioned, "You mustn't let the Judge know that I am off for a ride with my beau." She turned to my Uncle Shay with a twinkle in her eye.   "But Seamus will be our chaperone, won't you Seamus? So everything will be quite proper."   It took most of the kids a minute to figure out who Seamus was and then she actually giggled as we started for the door knowing that she was playing a game with herself as much as with us.

She was carefully placed in the middle of the back seat of the Chevy.   She was so tiny that, if she had been wearing gray instead of yellow she would have simply disappeared into the upholstery.   She looked straight ahead as we drove down the hill toward the county road.   My Uncle Shay drove and I sat in the front seat so that I felt a little like we had picked up a person stranded on the road, an actress maybe or someone on her way to a costume ball.   I was sad to think how out of place she looked, how time had seemed to go on without her like a poster I had seen once of Myrna Loy framed forever in a time to which she belonged.   The windows were partially down and when I turned to look at her, the ribbons waved about her shoulders and a single strand of hair had blown loose and floated in the sunlight.   She was still looking straight ahead of her and she smiled at me.

Without apparently taking any notice of where we were, she caught her brother's eye in the rear view mirror just in time to say, "I think, Seamus, I would like to go to Faribault so you should turn here."

Jane was the only one of her contemporary family members who had anything beyond a high school education.   She had attended a "normal" school in Faribault in preparation for becoming a school teacher. She must have had a good many memories about the small town, but on the drive there and even as we drove past her school and through the town, her hands remained clasped in her lap and her eyes remained focused straight ahead. She looked out the side window quickly and suggested,

"Perhaps we should stop for tea at the Grand, Seamus." My uncle looked a bit nervous when he had to tell her that the Grand was no longer there.

"Oh, my," she sighed, "How long ago, Seamus?"

"A long time, Janey. It closed many years ago."

"Of course," she said quietly, and took one quick look out the window before she returned to her statuesque pose. "Of course."

Again on the drive home she suggested, just in time for Uncle Shay to make the turn, that, perhaps, they should stop by the cemetery. I got a funny feeling when we pulled through the wrought iron gates and stopped just a few feet from where Lynn and I had stood not too long ago. Uncle Shay got out and lit his pipe while I helped my aunt from the car. She walked slowly and more than a little painfully, directly to her father's grave. Most of her family was buried here. Some underneath markers so old I could barely make out the inscriptions. We stood on a wide space in front of her father's marker that was free of any graves and suddenly I realized that we were standing on the very spot that would be her own burial plot. She must have felt me shiver because she patted my hand and hugged a little closer to me.

The evening had cooled off a little and a breeze

touched the top of the hill. My uncle brought the afghan and placed it around his sister's shoulders. I noticed that he let his arm rest there with the cover and that he was pressing his eyes tightly closed and open again.

We stood there for a long time, each thinking our own thoughts. I kept glancing over at the spot where I had discovered Lynn behind the tombstone. I felt the warmth of her against my hand and it startled me. And then I felt, even in the collected August heat, the cold hand resting on my arm. I could smell the cedar chips and lilac of my great aunt redolent of old hotel rooms and of my grandmother's vanity. I could also smell the metal of Lynn's flute and I could smell Lynn. Not of a perfume, but the smell of her. The smell of soap and perspiration and excitement.

When we finally turned to go, my uncle led his sister back to the car and I followed behind. They clung to each other a little tenaciously, I thought, and were slow to separate at the car. When we drove away, I found myself looking back, watching the gate disappear as we dipped down the hill, but Jane was looking straight ahead as though we had never stopped.

She insisted that I help her to her room. I got her settled on the edge of her bed and while she made a big production out of taking off her hat, Margreg and Bridey both talked at once asking questions and scolding all at the same time.

"Now, now, you two," she admonished. "I am much too tired right now for all this jabbering. Jackie will come back tomorrow and we'll tell you all about it.

Won't we, Jackie?"

"Yes, yes, do come back tomorrow, won't you?" I knew my Aunt Bridey was not the type who wanted to be left out of anything.

"Yes, I'll come back tomorrow." I said and I started to leave.

Jane turned to me, however, before I could say goodnight. She took both my hands in hers and I watched as a single tear cut a pinkish scar across her rouged cheek.

"You mustn't be afraid to go to the city, Jackie. You mustn't think that this is all there is."

"But Aunt Jane...," I started.

But she shook her head and interrupted.

"No. No, you have many, many more memories to make. There is nothing left here, Jackie. There is only your three old aunts who should have gone a long time ago."

I looked at all three of them as I held my Aunt Jane's hands. She looked at me and at Margreg and Bridey looked at me and we all nodded our heads like we had just signed a pact or something. My Aunt Mary came in to help Aunt Jane into bed.

"I always feel like I am interrupting some secret meeting when I walk in on you four. Why is that?"

"Because you are," said Margreg and she winked at me.

"Did you and Jackie have a nice drive, Jane?" she asked.

"Yes. Yes, a very nice drive. Next time Margreg and Bridget will have to join us. We'll do that very soon. Won't we, Jackie?"

I nodded as Aunt Mary ushered me to the door. I thought that would be very strange to see all three of them out driving.   But, of course, none of them ever went for another drive. None of them ever wanted to.

CHAPTER XII

Any man can lose his
hat in a fairy-wind

He sat beneath an ancient willow in a straight-backed chair.   Age and hard work drove him to the shade early each afternoon. It hadn't always been so. There was a time when day began for our hired man, Frank, before the sun came up and ended long after it had descended behind the rolling fields of corn.   Now he sat still looking up the dusty mile to the crossroads. His work-worn hands rested on the arms of his chair and his eyes did not waver. He did not really expect to see anything; yet, beneath the gray silence in his eyes there was a tiny glint of hope.   He watched the swirling phantom dust as though out of its wavering center she would appear, walking toward him. It was not the sadness of this daily routine that moved me, but the devotion he gave to a memory so long forgotten by others.

Frank Daly had lost the ability to do many things.

He could no longer withstand the long hours of heat. He could no longer ask his hands and his back to serve him as they had in the past. However, he remained to the day he died a remarkable teller of stories. Whether it was around the wood stove in Aunt Mary's kitchen, the warmth radiating off the glowing cast iron and mingling with the smells of fresh dough rising and hand-mixed pipe tobacco, or gathered on the back porch as the sun set and the farm settled gently to sleep, we never tired of the tales of people and events that had gone before us. He was a wonder and, as children, we could never get close enough to the man who knew the truth about every tree, every stream, every old maid in the county. Of all the stories he ever told, I believe I was the only one who heard the true story of Music Amber and I remain the only one who knows what really drew him to the spidery arms of the willow each early afternoon.

Frank had been the hired hand on our family farm for as long as any of us could remember. He had never married, never moved off to start a place of his own or a family of his own. He always said we were all the family he had and he counted himself lucky at that. My grandfather was fond of saying that family was at once our greatest joy and our eternal curse. I hadn't lived long enough at that point to understand the last part of his philosophy, but coming from an environment that was filled with the love and support of a large extended family, I certainly understood the part about being our greatest joy. Perhaps that is why I was so curious about Frank. My Aunt Jane, who knew every skeleton in every closet from Montgomery to the Iowa border, explained it her way.

"Frank was always a confirmed bachelor, Jackie, and if you let that go too long, time has a way of holding you to your commitment whether you like it or not." If she knew any more she wasn't telling and finally I decided that if I wanted to get the straight answer, I would have to go to the source. The prospect of moving away and never again seeing the family I loved in every way prompted me, I suppose, to be a bit more bold that last summer. Apparently the direct and simple approach is often the best because I got my answer on the first try.

I had been helping Frank chase an old sow into a second pen so we could get a good look at her piglets. The sow was determined to hold her ground and we were both sweat and mud from head to toe by the time we got her fenced off. Frank leaned against the rails and wiped hopelessly at his muddy face and hands. I climbed up on the fence next to him and scraped the muck off of my boots.

"How come you never got married, Frank? I mean, how come ya just stayed on here with us? We're all glad ya did. I was just wonderin..."

Frank wiped at his hands again and then walked over and picked up one of the squealing piglets. He checked its ears and pulled at its lips and thumped around checking for important pig information, whatever that was. I thought he was just going to ignore my question when he walked over and handed the frantic little pig to me.

"Let's call this one Pork Chop, what d'ya say? That way he'll know from his very first days that he's destined for the frypan. Kinda prepare the way, make it easier on 'im."

"O.K." I said as I dropped the pig, "Go on, Pork Chop, enjoy yerself while you can." We both laughed as Pork Chop ran squealing around the pen looking for his ma.   Then it was quiet and we swatted flies and scraped our boots and finally he looked at me and said,

~ ~ ~ ~

"I was a young man then, Johnny, so was yer dad and yer cousin Robert and we were, all three, hellions, I'll tell ya.   Now don't go tellin' yer dad I said so, but we traversed three counties here 'bouts just lookin' for good fun and more of it.   We started as close in as Kilkerry and often got clear over to Faribault and beyond.   Well, like all young pups, we never wanted that to end.   We were full of spit and vinegar and had no wish to be brung up short.   So we made a pact, the three of us.   One, no serious girlfriends.   Two, no serious thinking about havin' a serious girlfriend.   In short, nothing was to come between the three of us and the good fun we were enjoyin' together.   Well...we spit in our hands, shook all around, and the pact was made."

By this time we had made our way to the pump and had managed to get most of the mud off the important parts of us. Frank had stopped talking and I pulled my head out from under the pump and looked at him.   His hands were deep in his overall pockets and he was looking out between the barns toward the crossroads.   He started to walk toward the front yard and I followed silently behind him.

"Days have a way of flowin' one into the other, son, especially when you're livin' and lovin' every second of it. Well, it was like that I guess. Time just went on and we yipped and yapped and hollered our way across a number of years in that fashion. Until....."

He stopped and looked down at me, as if considering whether or not I should hear what he was about to tell. Then he settled himself on the lip of the front porch, looked off down the road, and went on.

"Yer dad had just gotten his hands on a 1934 Chev coupe," his eyes lit up with the memory, a grin spreading from ear to ear. "She was a spunky little thing that coupe. She bumped and jerked over them county roads like she was born just to serve the three of us. Well, it seemed like nothin' could stop us. We roared off into every sunset the good Lord could muster and crept on home with every sunup that followed."

Even at my age, I couldn't picture my grandfather tolerating that kind of behavior from his son, his nephew, and his hired man. But Frank was into another world now. He was the great teller of stories and he pulled me right in after him.

"On one such occasion," he continued, "we were headed over to Montgomery for a dance. We had spruced up and duded up and the four of us, Jimmy, Robert, the coupe, and me were six feet off the ground. It was Montgomery look out and mind your womenfolk."

He got very quiet then and seemed a little lost.

"So ya went to the dance," I encouraged, "and

whooped it up?"

"Oh, you bet we did. We danced the feet off everything that wore a skirt. And then, just about time to pack it in, I saw....I saw this young gal by the side door with a big grin on her face, lookin' right at me. She was sayin' a lot with that grin. She was sayin', 'Come on, Frank, ask me for the last dance.' She was sayin', "I dare ya ta walk over here and ask me'."

"So did ya?" I prompted, all impatience.

"Ya know, it's a funny thing, Johnny. I turned around thinkin' better of it, but that smile was still in front of me. Damned, if I didn't turn and march right over there. 'I'm Frank Daly', I says, 'and I'd like us ta dance'. 'I'm Music Amber', she says. 'and I thought you'd never ask'. We danced, all right. When I put my arm around her I thought she had slipped through my grasp, she was that slight. There didn't seem to be anything to her but a bit of dress and a smile that drew me around the dance floor like a magnet. Getting ahold of her was like trying to grasp a handful of foxfire on a hot summer night. Her dress just seemed to cling to me as it did to her as we whirled in circles through the yellow light. I felt like I had a butterfly in the palm of my hand and if I closed my fingers I would harm it or if I closed my eyes it would fly away. So I just watched her lips and tried to keep from getting dizzy. Even later when we walked through the fields, holdin' hands and talkin', I had the strange sense that I had dreamed her up. I don't even remember what happened to your dad and Robert or how we left the hall. I don't suppose this makes any sense, Johnny, but it was like I had stumbled into a magic dream. Not my dream but hers. There I was and I couldn't do anything about what would happen or for how long, because it wasn't my dream, ya see?"

He told me how they had ended up on the roof of an old hay shed in the middle of a field. And how they had talked all night 'til the sun came up.

"We talked about everything I'd been wantin' to talk about all my life. About how I was feelin' inside and how I had felt a long time ago. She talked about how she wanted sometimes to climb to the top of a very tall tree and spread out her arms and let the wind catch hold of her and carry her off across the sky. We didn't make love, ya know, like people might expect on that night. We just talked and then she said she had to go. When I said I'd see her home, her eyes got sorta empty. I don't know, like when ya look down a well after you've dropped a stone or something and all ya see is this kind of empty blackness. I remember getting real scared then and askin' if please, couldn't I see her ta home. Finally, when she said she'd come see me soon and that I was to watch for her comin' down the road, I felt a little better. So I watched her go off across the fields, disappearing into the rows of corn and morning sunlight."

As he pulled out his pocketknife and a plug of tobacco, I jumped up and looked myself toward the crossroads. I think I was as distressed as he was. "You mean you never saw her again? I mean, after that night she just disappeared?"

"Now what are you doin'? Tryin' to tell my story

for me?"

"No, I was just afraid..."

"So was I. So was I, Johnny. I came up by that willow over there every afternoon and looked down the road and every day that passed I got more and more sick at heart. Then, one afternoon I saw her walkin' toward me. I hadn't seen any cars comin' or anything. Suddenly there she was, walking away from the sun like she had been set down by the hand of the afternoon breeze. Sometimes she'd show up once a week, sometimes twice a week, and always the same way. When I least expected to see her there she was walkin' and wavin' at me. Robert and your dad had gotten sick of waitin' on me and of hearin' me talk about Music all the time, so they figured the pact was broken and they went their own way. I didn't care, ya see. I didn't care because all I wanted to do was see Music one more time, to be with her one more time, to try to hold her and feel her beside me one more time.

It was like that all that year. She would come walkin' down that road. I'd see her when the leaves were changin' and when the snow piled up six feet deep and when the lilacs bloomed. And every time I was with her it was better than the last and I had got so I was feelin' like it was a dream we shared together. I actually felt like I could hold her in my arms and feel her beneath me. But every time I asked her to stay, her eyes would empty again and she would leave with only the promise she would come back. Every time she left, I would try to find some trace of her, something I could hold onto. A piece of her dress or a hanky she had used or even a piece of straw she had chewed on and always there was nothing."

~ ~ ~ ~

I was afraid at this point in the story that I knew what would happen and I felt so sorry for Frank that I almost didn't want to hear the rest. But Frank was the consummate storyteller. He would not have let me escape without hearing the rest. He must have sensed, too, that he had led me to the turning point and so he toyed with me a bit. Instead of going on, he wandered off toward the edge of the hill, then sat in the chair beneath the old willow and looked out across the road. I sat down next to him and waited.

~ ~ ~ ~

"All that year I had never been happier. People said I was being foolish. They told me nobody had ever heard of Music Amber, that it was probably a made up name. They were quick to point out that if she made up her name, then what awful things might she have done that she had to hide? Your grandfather was mad at me most of the time, said I moped around like a sick pup and never got my work done. Well, it wasn't true what they said. I knew that and I didn't need to prove it. Then, just as summer was warming up, a week went by before I saw her and then maybe two weeks or three, so that by the end of the summer I hadn't seen her more than half a dozen times. All that winter I waited and she didn't come 'til spring. It got longer and longer between visits. Just when I was about to give up, she would come down the road again and my life would be full for a few hours or a few days or maybe a week. While I waited, I would try to imagine where she was and what she was doing. I would try to guess how she arrived out of the dust at the crossroad. And then one year she didn't come at all or the next or the next. The war came and I was gone from the farm for a long time. I wrote to her every week and asked your family to make sure she got the letters if she showed up. When I came home walking down that same road I had watched her walk so many times, I knew all those letters would be waiting for me."

"Were they, Frank? Were all the letters waiting for you?" He just nodded his head and I knew they had been and that she had never returned.

"So she never came back then."

"Oh, yes she came back. She had come back twice, she told me later. She had come back the last time, she said, to tell me she would stay. But I wasn't there and neither was your dad or Robert and nobody saw her, so that they could give her the letters."

There was a long pause as he collected himself.

"I saw her again in 1948 in Faribault. She was sittin' in a pickup truck with a whole passel of kids. All I saw was the smile and I leaned my head in the window and said, 'I'm Frank Daly and I'd like us ta dance'. She was holdin' a little girl, couldn't of been more 'an one or two and there was a little rise beneath her dress and I knew she couldn't dance. Not this time."

As I came toward Frank, sitting in his usual chair and looking toward the road, I knew why he looked into the afternoon sun. It wasn't, like most people thought, because he waited for Music Amber to materialize once again out of the past. He had waited for awhile after that time in Faribault, hoping that somehow fate would allow him to stumble back into her dream. But that hope had gone with the years.

"Let me put it to you this way, Johnny. Suppose you're standin" by an apple tree just loaded with bright, juicy apples and you know that each and every year that same tree will have more of the same. Why, you would pick one apple after another until you were full and then you'd go back for more. You would enjoy all the apples you cared to. Well now, let's say you stumble upon an apple tree and hanging there is one beautiful, bright, shiny apple. You know the tree will not bear again. Now, you pick that apple and you probably take your time enjoying each and every bite. When the apple is gone, and there are no prospects for any more, what have you got? Well, I'll tell you, because 'ol Frank Daly picked from that tree, and let me tell you, a short trip back to that tree, a look up into the branches, and the memory of that wonderful apple can recall a taste so sweet it can make the prospects of another long, hot day seem worth gettin' up for."

CHAPTER XIII

There was never a scabby sheep in a
flock that didn't like to have a comrade

It was Norman Rockwellian to the nth degree. Looking back, the entire town might well have been constructed by a production company as the location for their latest nostalgic-look-at-the-fifties movie. A visitor might expect to see the cast of American Graffiti or Happy Days or Stand By Me sipping sodas in the local malt shoppe while Meredith Wilson and a thousand and one trombones marched through the park across the street. It was, quite simply, what is now a cliche'. Of course, today no motion picture company would find the town as it once was. Instead they would find a commercially quasi-quaint annex to the north of St. Paul. They would have a difficult time filming their retrospective look at Mid America in the midst of a square block filled with shops designed to attract the attention of tourists and visitors anxious to spend their money on the cute and useless. It would be impossible for us to identify with a Ronny Howard strolling through the small town movie theatre now converted to a mini mall with chic boutiques, or enjoying a vegetarian croissant sandwich and a small salad of field greens and balsamic vinaigrette in the fashionable restaurant now occupying the old Post Office building at one end of the square. Even the few back alleys, crammed with cottage industries making and selling Irish knits and Swiss chocolate truffles, have become worldly.

As our oversized Packard cruised up old Highway 61, however, I was greeted by the original. Since we had pulled onto the tarmac that led toward the Twin Cities and away from the farm, I had stubbornly looked out of the back window. All that was important was behind me and I was not interested in what was ahead.

That morning I had knocked softly on the door to my great aunts' room hoping that they were still asleep and that I would not have to face them this last time before I left. They were all up, however, and insisted that I come in and say goodbye. There was much patting of my hands and moist eyes from Margreg and Bridey. When Aunt Jane set her cane aside and reached up to take my face in both her hands, I choked on my goodbye and hugged her close to me. I stepped away, looking uncomfortably at my feet not knowing how to make my exit. All three of them simply nodded their heads as if it were all over and nothing was left to be said. I closed the door behind me, walked through the kitchen to the car, and threw myself into the back seat. I didn't look back until we were well out of sight of the farm.   When I finally did turn around, it was too late to see everybody gathered at the top of the hill waving their farewells and calling their wishes that we return soon for a visit.   It was too late to see, one more time, the cluster of sun-soaked buildings that would forever have a strange hold on my memory.   I even missed Uncle Shay standing up on the old Johnny Popper and waving a tribute from my early obsession.   My father honked and pointed to the field, but I clenched my eyes tight and forced my lower lip out even further.   I was not too late to see Lynn standing at the cross-roads her hands stuffed as usual deep into the back pockets of her jeans.   I managed a small wave and she waved back and a kind of forced smile appeared and was quickly gone.   When we were finally on the highway I turned, rested my elbows on the back of the seat, and watched the road unroll in a waving black strip behind us.

Highway 61 and the railroad tracks ran north out of St. Paul to Duluth passing us just on the edge of our business district.   Immediately to the east was the town square complete with a Post Office building at one end and a statue of our own World War I hero at the other.   The interesting thing about the statue of old Milton T. Whistle was that there was no Whistle family in town and nobody could find any record of there ever being a Whistle family in town.   Once or twice a year some group or other would write a letter to the editor claiming that the local war hero was not really local at all and there would be a big hoopla for a few weeks until something more important captured everyone's attention.   We came close to losing Milton on one occasion when one of the many women's clubs gathered support for replacing Milton T. with a statue of Winowachee, a legendary giant Indian whose angry footprint had made the indentation that formed our lake. The local American Legion fought tooth and nail, however, and Milton T. Whistle was lucky enough to survive many more years of civic groups and pigeon droppings.

The main portion of the business district really only centered on one square block.   But within that square block we managed to include everything that, in later years, became a cliche'. There was the local barber, of course, who had four ways of cutting hair, short, very short, shorter still, and shaved. The Ben Franklin and the Coast to Coast were side by side.   In fact, we had one of everything that was needed.   A grocery store, liquor store, meat market, bakery, jeweler, etc. Our real claim to double cliche' fame was that we had, not one, but two movie theaters and two malt shoppes.   One block east of Main Street was the National Guard Armory. The war trucks had rolled out of that armory only once that I remember.   The Rice Street gang had made plans for a rumble with our local toughs.   They were to meet in the square on a Friday night to settle their differences.   Actually, they were so much alike, it was difficult to imagine that they had any differences but apparently they invented some, because the confrontation took place replete with switchblades, chains, zip guns, and menacing grins. Those of us who had gathered in safety across the street to cheer on the mayhem and bathe our hands vicariously in blood were disappointed when the trucks rolled up and the combat ready teenagers in fatigues intimidated the combat ready teenagers in leather.

The business district was seven or eight blocks from the lakeshore. This, of course, was the more affluent residential area of town. All of the names that were important names could be found housed on the lake side of town, in large old houses with wide, screened-in porches. The neighborhoods gave off that solid, comfortable feeling that made people want to smile and dream as they strolled between street lamps on summer nights. The light, too, that radiated from the winter windows of these homes seemed somehow just a little warmer, a little more inviting than those on the other side of town. When the Lord said, "Thou shalt not covet thy neighbor's goods," these were the neighbors He was talking about.

To the west of the highway and the tracks was the more modest residential area.

Maybe six blocks after crossing the tracks, my father turned off Fourth Street and onto a dirt road that took us one block further to a row of six houses all exactly the same except for the color and the degree of progress toward landscaping. Directly across from us and for several blocks around there was nothing but vacant fields. Within a few years the neighborhood would develop a character of its own. Trees would grow, additions to houses would alter their common shape and give them some individuality, a school would be built nearby, and more houses would eventually be added. On that first day in

September, however, the tract home and everything that went with it made me feel sick to my stomach and utterly alone. I sat on the front stoop with my knees curled up to my chest blocking everybody's way as they tried to unpack the car and get us settled in our new home. My sister came running out screaming about all the neat things we had like hot running water and electric light switches, and a toilet that flushed, but I wasn't interested. Actually, I was, but if you set yourself into a good pout you're forced to stay with it or people will think you weren't sincere from the start. It's a child's Catch 22 and probably the reason adults abandon it as a viable choice of behavior.

I was about to relent and go inside the house when I caught sight of a boy standing in the front yard next door. He was wearing brown high-water cords, a white t shirt and socks, and brown penny loafers. His reddish hair was neatly combed. His shiny clean face was filled with freckles that ran to splotches and you could see that his shoes had been recently shined. I got the impression that his clothes had been pressed down to his underwear and knew, without being able to see, that his fingernails were clean. It was a look that my mother would try in vain to duplicate in me. I had a cowlick that refused to stay down no matter how many little dabs I used, an overbite that was soon to encounter an orthodontist, and a propensity for always looking a little scruffy. Even after my Saturday night bath, all decked out in my Sunday best, I wouldn't look as neat and tidy as the boy who stood and stared at the new kid on the block. He finally sidled across the driveway that separated our two yards, brushed some nonexistent dirt from his knees and said, "Movin' in?"

Had I been witty beyond my years, I might have said something like, "No, we just spend our weekends carrying stuff in and out of vacant houses," or "Naw, we're going to abandon my sister here, but we want to make it look good for the neighbors." Instead I simply said, "Ya."

I must have said it about the way I felt about it, because he was quick to be reassuring. "I just moved here about a year ago. From Peoria. Know where that is?"

I shook my head. One of my greatest fears was that I was going to be taken for a dumb hick and here it was. I couldn't answer the first question I had been asked.

"Ya, well, it's in Illinois." He pronounced the 's' on the end so that it sounded like 'noise'. "This is a pretty neat neighborhood, lots a kids and all. We play ball in the lot across the street. What school ya goin' to?"

When he mentioned ball my eyes lit up and I stood to take a closer look at the vacant lot. I could see the vague outline of a diamond and a chicken wire back stop. I loved baseball and for the moment I forgot my moodiness and started to take a good look around. I was about to ask him his name and when they might be getting a game together when his father came out of the house and hollered for him. "Tom? Tom, come on. I wanta get right back."

"I gotta go. Confession. I mean ta church with my dad. So...see ya."

He and his father were starting down the street when he turned and hollered at me, "We're playin' kick the can after dark. Come on out. Bring your sister too. See ya."

At first there were just a few of us gathered in the middle of the block. By the time the streetlights came on, however, I realized that Tom had not exaggerated about there being a lot of kids in the neighborhood. There must have been twenty-five or thirty of us by the time the game got underway.

Kick the can is just one of the many variations on hide and seek that exist all over the country. An empty can is placed in a strategic spot, say under the streetlight at the corner, and one person is chosen to be "it." The person who is "it" closes his eyes and counts to a hundred while everybody else scatters in a mad scramble to find the best hiding places. In this case, however, the "it" person doesn't just find you, tag you, and recruit you to find the rest. As a matter of fact, if he finds you, he tries not to let on but runs back to the can and calls you in from your hiding place. The object for the person hiding is to anticipate that he has been discovered and run back to the can before the person who is "it" can get there. If you get there first, you can kick the can and, while the "it" person goes after it, find another hiding place. The more captures the "it" person gets the more difficult it becomes to kick the can. The last person found wins the game. After the first night, I must have played that game a thousand times and I never knew there to be a winner. Most of us got impatient hiding and would rather be involved in the hunt. Some, like Joey

Pentellio, were obstinate hiders. Pentellio claimed to be the only person ever to have won a game, but that was simply because he had buried himself under the garbage in Mr. Lawson's trashcan for four hours. When he finally came out and declared himself the winner, the rest of us had been home in bed for an hour.

That first night was a test for my sister and me. I suppose we knew it was. Our parents had to force us out the door saying the best way to get settled was to meet new friends. With some kind of sixth sense, the leaders decided when everybody who was going to show was there and the game started. A mean looking kid who was half bald at fifteen and wore grimy looking jeans and combat boots looked at me and said, "Let the new kid be 'it'."

"Hey, that's not fair. He doesn't even know our names. He..."

"Shut up, Gretchen," said the bald kid. "You're 'it' and Gretch can help ya with the names."

You were supposed to count as loud as you could so people could hear you and know you weren't cheating. By the time I got to twenty, the night was quiet. All I could hear were the crickets and a radio playing accordion music somewhere off in the dark. The boundaries had been decided earlier, so I just started to walk around checking bushes and trees and dark corners. I wanted to do well, show them how fast I could run, how well I would fit in. Gretchen walked behind me snapping her gum and calling someone, the bald kid I suspected, a stupid Fart Breath. She couldn't have been more than ten. She had the whitest hair I'd ever seen that shot out of her head in silky wisps. The rest of her disappeared in the darkness so that she appeared to be a grotesque head floating along four feet off the ground behind me.

"Any ideas where I should look, Gretchen?" I asked.

"I ain't givin away no hiding places. Just names. That's all Fart Breath said I had to do."

"Well, then, we could be out here for hours before I find anybody."

"I can't. I gotta get home pretty soon...AHHH!!" She screamed just as the bushes in front of us exploded. I was off, like beating the throw to first might mean the game. I was tearing toward the light at the end of the block while whoever jumped out of the bush pressed at my heels. I heard Gretchen yell frantically behind me.

"It's Clancy. Clancy!"

"Thanks," I gasped as I flung myself toward the shiny tin can in the middle of the street. If I could just get one of them, the rest would be easy. This first one was important.

Gretchen was still calling "Clancy" behind me. I skidded to a stop, my foot planted on top of the can.

"Clancy," I hollered, "I call in Clancy." From every bush, shed roof, window well, and tree branch in the whole block came whoops, catcalls, yells, and uproars of laughter. Clancy lay a foot away from the tin can, his tongue dripping, his tail wagging.

It went from bad to worse as I ran for the can time after time, only to have it kicked into the night. The taunts and laughter kept echoing around the neighborhood with an occasional "Clancy" shouted out of the darkness, and then the jeers would grow louder and the mocking laughter would increase. When they had finally had their fun and I was totally humiliated, my mother topped things off by being the first to holler out the back door that it was time to come in. As hiding places were abandoned and people started to drift toward their homes, my sister came up beside me and took my hand.

"Come on, Jack, we gotta go in." I gave the can a swift kick myself and started for the house. Tom came running up behind us.

"Hey, where you guys goin'?"

"We gotta go in," I said.

"Aw, ask if ya can stay out a little longer. We're gettin' together at Chamber's for cocoa and stuff."

I looked at my sister. "But....I thought..."

"Great game, huh? Best we've had in a long time. Hey...you're not mad, are ya? I mean we always do that when it's someone's first time."

"Do what?"

"You know, Chrome Dome hiding right there so he could beat ya to the can every time." My sister was laughing and I realized that even she had been in on it.

"Did you know about Fart Breath, too?" I asked.

"Who?"

"My brother," said Gretchen from behind us. "Old Fart Breath. Come on, you guys, before he eats all the good stuff."

As we walked into the Chamber's kitchen, a big cheer went up and the memory of Kilkerry slipped away just a tiny fraction. I had spent most of that day staring out the back window of our car and believing that the life I was leaving behind was the only life I would ever have. Once again, I had been looking in the wrong direction.

CHAPTER XIV

If God sends you down a stoney path
may He give you strong shoes

We were having an Indian war. That's what old man Druffel would holler at us from his front porch as we passed by. He always had this big bath towel tied around his neck like a bib that covered the whole front of him almost down to the plaid slippers that came up over his ankles and tied like giant booties. A red stocking cap was crammed down over his ears, whether it was July or January. Tom Lawson said that Druffel was just like a baby and that he wore diapers and everything. There were a lot of cruel jokes whenever Mrs. Druffel hung out her sheets or when she took her husband uptown with her and tied him up to the parking meter while she did her shopping.

"Indian Summer is battling it out with White Man Winter." He'd holler. Then he would laugh and giggle and flap his towel at us as we hurried by.

"Whose gonna' win?" He'd yell after us, "I'll bet

on the White Man. I'll bet on the White Man!"

Underneath all the jokes and bravado, we were all scared of him. On days when I wasn't in a hurry, or if I was riding my bike, I would go around the block the other way just to avoid having to pass by the Druffels' place. Two days before Halloween, Mrs. Druffel would begin making caramel apples and popcorn balls. She would wrap them in waxed paper and tie red and green Christmas ribbon around them to keep them fresh and on Halloween night she would set them by the front door on a long tray and turn on the porch light so the children wouldn't stumble. She loved to see all the different costumes the mothers had made and she would tell her husband about the ghosts and goblins and hoboes and witches and clowns that would come to their door for trick or treats. But the doorbell never rang at the Druffels' on Halloween. None of us had the courage to overcome our fear of the "crazy" who lived there even though we would take almost any risk to obtain more treats. The following day Mrs. Druffel would put all of the caramel apples and all the popcorn balls into bags and drive to the children's hospital and tell her husband that next year, perhaps, the children would come to their door.

Although none of us knew what "Indian War" the old man was talking about, it didn't keep us from enjoying the late summer. When the sun went down in molten lava, the edges of the clouds scorched pink as they ran in streaks away from its heat, the nip in the air would remind us that sweaters and coats would be out of mothballs soon. But during the day, we were still in our shirt sleeves trying not to let school interrupt our extended summer fun.

The short cut to school took me past the Druffels' at the end of our block, through Benton's woods, across an empty lot, around the Geonettis' garage and out their driveway, across the street, around the edge of "the swamp"(nothing more than a low spot that collected rain water and the neighbor's grass clippings), down the block, through the Apples' backyard, into the back lot of Kline's grocery store, and across the street to school. The path was taken by everybody who lived west of the school and it was well worn. When winter came, most of the short cut was abandoned in favor of what we called the "castle walk." The snowplows would push the snow up at the side of the road in huge drifts. After the plow had passed, people would shovel their driveways, piling the snow even higher on both sides of their drives. Out of this innocent-looking phenomenon fifty or so school kids created a winter battlement from the edge of town to St. Mary's Grade School. Walking across the drifts created an icy path that rose up like a turret at each side of the driveways and on each corner. In between was a relatively flat top to the rampart. The challenge came as long icy slides were created at either end of the turrets. After several good snowfalls, we could walk across the rampart six or seven feet off the ground and slide fifteen feet or more from the top of one of the turrets.

I was running late, as usual, on what promised to be another unseasonably warm day in October. I didn't have time to avoid old Mr. Druffel and it was easy to explain to myself why I ran by his house without having to admit that I was frightened by his bizarre behavior and the weird look of him. He hollered anyway and waved his towel like he was throwing rice at a wedding. I was halfway through Benton's woods before his voice faded and I stopped to tie my shoe. I had just started up again when I saw Dave Nordinger and Gretchen Turdle join the path from another direction.

"Hey, Nordie, Turd," I hailed, never wanting to travel to or from school alone if it could be avoided. We seldom called each other by first names. It was always the last name or some variation on it. It was pretty easy to tell how people felt about you by the way they said your name. Shortening the name to something familiar was friendly and could even, between sexes, be like an endearment. Twisting the last name to something new was often insulting, even challenging. My own name seemed difficult to shorten, but it often became Laney Haney or Lanney Fanny. Mostly it was just Laney. Whether this was peculiar to our town, I don't know, but even after almost thirty years when I returned to visit my old home the first person I saw from the old group greeted me by my last name and, come to think of it, I greeted him the same way.

Nordie and Turd stopped and waited for me and as we came out the far end of the woods we ran into half the neighborhood. They were standing around with their bookbags, lunch boxes, and serious faces like they were planning a break from Alcatraz. Chrome Dome Turdle, Gretchen's brother, was standing on top of a stump gesticulating wildly with his dirty hands, pleading with the indifferent crowd to join him in shoving it to the Sisters in St. Joseph. Actually it was the Sisters of St. Joseph but Chrome Dome liked his little twist better. He proposed that the way to "stick it to them" would be to stay away from school. Since this was Friday, he reasoned, by Monday they would have forgotten about it and if we all stuck together what could they do, anyway?

Tom Lawson was standing like a stork polishing the tip of his loafer on the back of his calf and idly tossing a football in the air while Gordy Masters, better known as Masterbater, tried to light the fag stuck in the corner of his mouth. He had seen someone in a movie strike a wooden match by lifting his leg and running it across his thigh. The little pile of broken matches next to him proved at least that he didn't give up easily. The others mostly kicked dirt with their toes and looked anxiously toward school. It wouldn't be long now and the decision of whether or not to skip school would be a moot question. Any minute now Sister Barbara would step out on the steps and ring the black-handled, brass bell that sat on the pedestal at the feet of the Blessed Virgin. Actually the Virgin could be found in both of the main halls upstairs and downstairs and in every classroom as well. The brass bell, however, sat at the feet of the largest Virgin, which was located just outside of Sister Barbara's office. Anyone attempting to touch the bell would be seen by two Virgins, one of whom was alive and weighed well over two hundred pounds.

Nobody was really listening to Turdle, but each of us had our own reasons for wanting to play hooky.

While Chrome Dome ranted about group subversive action, the rest of us weighed the possible punishment against the benefits of taking the day off. The morning sun was already warm and I for one knew that I didn't want to face "The Bird Woman" on a beautiful day like this. Our eighth grade teacher was Sister Clara Williams. Her love of birds and her constant attempts to foster in us a similar fondness won her the nick-name "Bird Woman." She was a very tall woman with a more than average sized nose that protruded past her wimple. When she moved about the room she unconsciously copied the rhythms of her favorite species. When she raised her arms and the folds of her habit unfurled like wings, there was no doubt left in our minds that either she had been a bird in her past life or she was about to become one in the next.

Just as it looked as though we were all going to make the same decision, Lewis Herbert jumped up and, holding his briefcase in one hand and his lunch box in the other, he bolted down the path like a frightened rabbit. After about twenty yards he turned and screamed back at us, "You guys are gonna get in big trouble. You wait and see. You just wait." With that off his chest, he continued his frantic race to beat the ringing of the bell.

"Come back here, you little rodent!" Yelled Chrome Dome, but to no avail. Lewis was one of three brothers in the Herbert family. His older brother was called House probably because he was so large. Lewis, himself, was nicknamed Mouse mostly because of the wire-rimmed glasses he wore pressed on the bridge of his pointy nose and Randal, his younger brother, was Worm. Randal was a very nice little kid and had no obvious wormlike characteristics, but the name stuck even through high school.

"You all know Mouse is gonna tell," Lawson shifted legs and polished his other shoe.

"He's gonna give TwoTon Barbara all our names and then she's gonna call our moms and the shit's gonna hit the fan."

"He's not gonna tell," Gretchen was standing in the back of the crowd, her arm around a skinny little fifth grader. "The Worm is with us," she said as she hugged our smiling hostage closer. "He ain't gonna rat on his own brother."

The faint sound of a bell came over the roof tops and we knew our decision was irrevocable. We were in big trouble now just for being tardy, so there was no point in not going all the way and skipping the whole day. Now that we were free, the problem was what to do with the day. It didn't take us long to realize that we couldn't be seen anywhere and that meant staying away from uptown, from the park, from the beach, and from everybody's house. That didn't leave too many exciting choices. We had just about decided that Nordie would sneak home for his Monopoly game and that we would stay in the woods until school was out. I never won at Monopoly. Somehow, I always ended up with all the utilities and the railroads while everybody else stacked up rows of houses and hotels. Besides, I thought, it might be safer if we got a little further away.

"If we hid out for a little while," I suggested, "we could catch the nine o'clock bus into St. Paul and then we could do whatever we wanted until this afternoon."

"Great idea, Laney," said Chrome Dome in his most sarcastic tone. "and how the hell we gonna pay, huh?"

"Today is Pagan Baby Day, right? Hasn't everybody got their money for a pagan baby? That should be more than enough for bus fare."

"Ya, and I got my milk money too." Randal held up his fifty cents. "For the week."

Gladys Cooper was one of those people who always does the right thing. She never even seemed tempted to go the least bit astray. It was no surprise that as we started to make our plan, she had the only objection.

"We can't spend the pagan baby money on the bus, you guys. Those little babies are counting on us to buy them."

Everybody looked over at Gladys as though she had just stepped off a flying saucer. It wasn't so much that she had said something. It was more the shock of realizing she was there at all.

"Why aren't you in school, Gladys?" Lawson asked as though he were her father.

She drew herself up even straighter than usual, pushed her glasses up on the bridge of her nose with her index finger, and explained as though she were talking to a group of peasants.

"I am willing to go along with playing hooky because we are all together for the day, but I will not spend my pagan baby money on my own pleasure."

A whole chorus of jeers and catcalls and name-calling followed.

"OOOH, parr...don me, your Goodliness."

"Little Miss GoodyTwoShoes!!"

"Alright! Alright!" I said, "Nobody has to go who doesn't want to."

But Chrome Dome was adamant. "Look. We stick together today. If we decide to go downtown, we all go. Gretch, give Cooper your milk money so she can save a pagan baby and let's get goin'"

"Give her yer own milk money, Fart Breath," said his sister.

"Never mind," Gladys said, "I have enough of my own, but the rest of you had better have some more money by Monday or..."

"Or what, Cooper?"

"Or else......or else those little babies starve to death."

We decided that we would wait on the edge of the woods until just before the bus came, then we would make our way across the street and into the bushes by the bus stop until we saw it coming down the street.

"Forget it, Lanny Fanny," Nordie was not happy and he was voicing the concern of the rest of them as well. "Those bushes are in Druffel's backyard. I ain't goin' anywhere near that place. That guy's a nut, man. Forget it!"

"It will only be for a couple of minutes, Nordie. And besides, he's always out on the front porch, not out back."

After a few minutes of haggling, the plan was settled. There were about twelve of us so we decided it would be best to tell the bus driver it was a field trip and that we were meeting our teacher downtown, a plan that had a million holes, but it sounded good to us. We sat around soaking up the morning sun, glad we weren't in school, trying to concentrate on getting downtown instead of getting caught. While we waited, I leaned over to give Gladys some encouragement because she was studiously going through her pocketbook, only to learn my first lesson in personal ethics.

"Hey, listen, Cooper," I whispered, "Nobody knows how much you were going to give for the pagan baby, so if you need to spend half you'll still have half left and nobody will be the wiser. See, nobody 'ill know."

She slowly took off her glasses and cleaned them with her shirttail as she looked down her nose at me. She was already good at playing the self-righteous little feminist she would eventually become. "I would know, Jackie." She was the only person outside my family that called me Jackie and she always used it when she wanted to put me in my place. "I would know and that's all that's important."

I was glad that our fearless leader, Chrome Dome, thought it was time to make for the bushes in Druffel's back yard. We had to go in twos and threes so that we were less conspicuous. Gladys and I were the last two across. We were making our way along the side of the house and toward the bushes where the others waited, when he started hollering.

"Boy! Girl!" He yelled as he flapped his towel, "Boy! Girl! Come...Over...Now!" I froze in my tracks and grabbed Gladys's arm, afraid that he had alerted the whole neighborhood, which included all of our mothers and several fathers, and that meant big trouble.

"Boy! Mamma sick. Lady sick. Look! Look!"   I turned to look and so did Gladys.   He had stopped waving his towel and was holding out his hand towards us, palm up, clutching and unclutching his fist.   "Boy! Girl!"

"Laney, Cooper!" hissed Chrome Dome.   "Get over here, you shit-for-brains, the bus is coming. Forget that nut! Get over here!"

I started for the bushes again, but Gladys pulled on my arm.

"He's calling to us, Jackie. He looks like he needs help."

I could hear the bus coming now and the rest of the kids hissing and screeching at us to hurry up. Gladys took my hand and pulled me toward the front porch as the bus whooshed by and Chrome Dome stamped his feet and pounded himself on the head. "Christ! I don't believe it!" He wailed.

The old man was waving his towel again and smiling at us. Gladys pushed me up on the porch. He put out his hand like he wanted to shake hands saying over and over, "Nice boy. Nice girl. Help Momma," and pointing toward the front door. I put Gladys between us and went to the screen door.

"Mrs. Druffel?" I called into the darkness. "Mrs. Druffel, is everything O.K.?" When there was no answer, I looked over at Gladys who motioned me to go inside.   The rest of the kids had gathered at the end of the porch, staring dumbfounded at our audacity.   I couldn't see anything right away because all the curtains were drawn.   I called for Mrs. Druffel and Gladys, who had followed me in, called out as well, but there was no answer.   I heard a clock ticking on the mantel and what sounded like the whistle of a teapot coming from the kitchen.

"Maybe she's out back," I whispered over my shoulder and I started for the back of the house.   I heard Gladys gasp and I turned.   She had her hands to her mouth and was staring wide-eyed at the floor in front of the slipcovered couch.

"Is she hurt?" I blurted out not knowing what to think.

"I...I don't know.   She..Mrs. Druffel?   Mrs. Druffel?"

"Maybe we'd better call someone," I said. "I'll call someone."   I looked around for the phone, but I couldn't think.

"The kitchen."

"What?"

"The kitchen," Gladys said. "Maybe the phone's in the kitchen."

I didn't know what else to do, so I called my mother.   By the time she got down the street, the ambulance she had called was already there.   As police, firemen, and ambulance drivers got in each other's way, Gladys and I stood on the front porch and watched in silence.   When they wheeled Mrs. Druffel past us, I realized that Mr. Druffel was standing between us holding each of our hands.   He smiled and nodded to everyone who passed.   Both Gladys and I noticed that no one appeared to be in any hurry and when the ambulance pulled out into Fourth Street, the siren was silent.

When my mother came out to get him, Mr. Druffel would not let go of our hands so we had to go inside with him. All three of us sat on the couch while my mother went around opening drapes and pulling up shades. It was pretty obvious that Mr. Druffel had just messed his pants, but I didn't say anything.

"What's gonna happen, Mom?"

"Happen, Jackie?"

"You know, I mean to him?"

"Well, Dr. Druffel's sister is coming from Minneapolis. She's going to take the doctor to her home for awhile. After that, I don't know, Jackie."

"Doctor?" Gladys asked, incredulous. "You mean, like a scientist like...you know...a...ah...mad...?"

"No. I mean like a pediatrician. A children's doctor. Doctor Druffel practiced here for many years before he became ill. Now why don't you two run along and make the best of the rest of the day." She turned to look at us with her hands sternly on her hips. "Since you were good enough to help Mr. Druffel, I guess I'll make the call to Sister Barbara." As we started to go, he called out to us. "I'll bet on the White Man."

"Me, too." I said.

"Me, too. Me, too," he agreed happily and waved his towel as we left.

As we joined the rest of the kids and started toward uptown, Gladys tugged on my arm and asked. "Why do you think she took care of him all this time? Why didn't she just put him away someplace? Who would have blamed her? Who would of thought it was wrong?"

"She would. I think she would have thought it was wrong. And I suppose that's all that's important. Right, Gladys?"

CHAPTER XV

*Young people don't know what old age is,
and old people forget what youth was*

Each new day at school, each new neighborhood adventure and each new friend pushed the farm and my life there a little further away. I was slowly becoming more of a town boy than a farm boy even if I didn't see it as such.

I did it on a dare. I suppose the others followed because we had become friends and because whatever one of us did the others just naturally tagged along. We were all a little different, a little lost, and more than a little frightened of being left out. It was easy for the stronger, more self-assured groups to manipulate us. Because we were usually the last ones to be picked by team captains, the first to be shoved or pushed, and the brunt of everybody's jokes, we developed a fierce sense of loyalty. I remember a few earlier friends, like Melvin Hobson, and more recent friends are in sharper focus but the memory of those five friends is unique. It is a bit more pain-filled and, because of our desperate need for each other, a bit more wonderful too. I was glad they agreed to go along with me on that night and just a little less frightened.

It was Friday afternoon. We had put homework out of our minds until Sunday night and had gathered at the Malt Shoppe for platters of french fries and to see what we could do about what promised to be a boring weekend. We were crammed into our usual booth, second from the front with a good view of the front door. We always sat in the same spot, the result of some kind of pecking order, I suppose, though I didn't think about it at the time. Gretchen Turdle sat with her brother Chrome Dome and Davey Nordinger with their backs to the door but a good command of the rest of the room. Gladys Cooper, myself, and Eddie "The Mole" Halverson sat on the other side with Gladys pushed against the inside corner and The Mole on the outside so that, as he put it, he wouldn't get "cloisterphobia." The french fries were hand sliced and saturated with grease so that the salt clung to each potato like a sugar glaze. The ketchup either lay in a reddish mud puddle at the end of the platter or was poured in thick red rivers across the top depending on aesthetic taste. The Mole and I were of the red river group which annoyed Gladys.   She tried to pull "undamaged" fries out of the pile and dip them carefully on the tip before she made them soggy and disgusting by sucking off the salt before she ate them. There was no hassle on the other side of the table. All three of them liked "virgin fries" free of both salt and ketchup.

The Mole was into one of his "what a sorry bunch of losers the rest of us were" lectures. Eddie was actually pretty popular. He was a star baseball player and looked closer to normal than the rest of us. His sister, Mary Jo, was the most popular girl in school. Every guy I knew lusted after her but, of course, they never mentioned that to The Mole. "If you guys are gonna' sit around making your usual stupid plans which turn out to be no kind of plan at all, I'm quits. I'm goin' to Deiter's party. I think we should all go to Deiter's party."

Chrome Dome licked his fingers and looked across at Eddie, "We ain't invited, Halverson. We're never invited to Deiter's parties. Besides, Deiter's got that assma. His chest is square and he wheezes all the time. Drives me crazy."

The Mole just looked at Chrome Dome like he was some kind of strange vegetable that talked. "Dome...you are a dumb fuck, ya know that?"

"Ya?"

"Ya!"

It was Gretchen as usual who stepped in and held her brother in check. "Will you shut up, Fart Breath. Why do you two have to go at it all the time. We're making a plan so let's make a plan."

"What da ya want us to do, Halverson?" I asked. "Crash Deiter's dumb party? We'll just get in trouble."

"Ooooo! Well, we wouldn't want to get in trouble. Oh, no. That might be too much fun. Even normal. Ya know, the trouble with you guys is you spend half your time talkin' about how weird everybody else is.

Have you ever looked around this table.   Go ahead!
Take a good look!"

The conversation came to a stop as Kathy
Heffelman walked by.   Her breasts were so big it
looked like she laid a watermelon sideways across her
chest.   She always wore bulky knit sweaters and you
could see her colored bras underneath.   When she was
cold or excited the nipples poked through the knit like
she had pasted little jaw breakers on the ends.   The
Mole opened his mouth dripping a french fry on his
pants.   He was trying to dab at the ketchup stain and
still keep an eye on Kathy.

"That's disgusting, Eddie." Gladys said.

"Disgusting? She's the one with the jugs, not
me."

Right behind Kathy came Gordy Masters.   He had
stuffed a three-ring binder under his shirt and was
mimicking her walk.   The whole place was in an uproar
but Kathy was used to it and just kept going.   Learning
to live with humongous tits must build character.   I
was hoping Masters would keep going.   He always
delighted in giving one or all of us a bad time and I
knew that if he stopped it would be my day to get it.
Unfortunately, he did stop.   A quick opening from
Nordie gave Gordy that much more of a reason to razz
me.

"Hey, Masterbater. Want a french fry? You could
go play with it."

"Nordinger! Lend me a fag."

"Sorry. I don't smoke."

"Laney! Got a fag?"

I handed him one of my Pall Malls just because it

was interesting to watch the ritual of Masters smoking. Many of us smoked simply because we thought we should and subconsciously we fought the whole process. Masters was at home with a cigarette. He rested the cigarette on his fingers, then slapped the palm of his hand and the slender cigarette flipped up and into the corner of his mouth. It was very cool. People begged him to do it all the time. From then on, however, it was a serious business. He lit the cigarette with a kitchen match struck along his thigh. After that, it never left his mouth. He inhaled, sucking the smoke down to his toes, then let it trickle back out his nose as he talked. I never saw him take it out of his mouth. It burned red hot all the way down to his lips before he took the tip of his tongue and forced it out onto the ground.   The process caused him to constantly squint his right eye against the rising smoke. It gave him a sinister or sexy look depending on which way he used it.   This particular time he wanted to look sinister as he raked me over the coals for my less than heroic behavior that morning.

"So, Laney. I hear you peed your pants this morning and had to go home at recess and change. Bouck...bouck...bouck."

I hadn't really peed my pants. I'll admit there was a slight loss of control but I didn't actually pee my pants.   Richard Hawkins bullied me around a bit because I had called him a cheater. He didn't hit me that hard but my lips got cut on my braces and there was a lot of blood. It was over in a hurry. Quick, humiliating and typical of my fighting ability.

"Laney, you're such a chicken. How can you guys

hang around with such a chicken?"

"Jackie is not a chicken. As a matter of fact I have seen him be very brave." I slid a little lower in my seat cursing Gladys for coming to my defense.

"Jackie? Oh, I'm sorry, Jackie, for calling you a chicken in front of your girlfriend."

"She's not my girlfriend." It seemed it was my day to be a real chicken. I should have punched him in his big mouth.

"O.K., that's enough, Masters." Eddie said. "Get lost will ya."

Gordy had had his fun and it would have ended there if Chrome Dome hadn't opened his fat lips.

"Yah. At least Laney isn't afraid of ghosts and goblins. He isn't afraid of the dark like some weenies I know." The Dome was joined in his laughter by everyone within earshot. Everybody had heard about Masters' run-in with the Hogerty ghost.

Apparently Gordy Masters had used his sexy look on some girl at the movies. He was walking her home stopping every block or so to fondle her and hoping to find a place where they could get down to some serious petting. They were almost to her house when desperation drove them into the weeds at the edge of the swamp at the end of the lake. Gordy was a fast mover and we all agreed that they were probably slashing their naked bodies to pieces on swamp grass and cattails when the ghost appeared. Just as they were about to become one with the swamp, Gordy heard a howling noise and looked up. All the girl remembers is that Gordy let out a blood curdling scream, pointed toward the middle of the swamp , and went tearing off into the night leaving the girl and his pants behind.

"You don't know what yer talkin' about, Chrome Dome."   Masters had released the hot butt from the corner of his mouth and had turned back to our booth with fear in his eyes.   "I know what I saw and what I heard. I saw it. It was there for real."

"Ya? Well, like I said, there's chickens and then there's chickens, Masterbater. People who live in glass houses and all that shit. Ya know."

Masters slunk off toward the back of the room followed by our hoots and laughter, but as we crossed the park headed for home we all knew that he was partially right.   All in all we were pretty dull and seldom took a risk any greater than sneaking in the back door of the movie theatre.   It was while we were sitting in the park at the foot of our local war hero, Milton T. Whistle, that the idea came to me.

The plan was simplicity itself.   We would wait 'til dark, make our way unseen into the park and proceed to the foot of Milton T. Whistle and begin removing the eight bolts that held his bronze likeness to the pedestal.   When I outlined the plan to the others, even The Mole forgot about Deiter's party.   We made a list of everything we would need and assigned each person's responsibility before we arranged the rendezvous for later that night.

By nine o'clock Davey Nordinger and I were behind the Post Office with Gretchen and The Mole, Gladys and Chrome Dome were across the highway at the train depot. Everything was closed on Main Street except Kohler's Malt Shoppe and the Movie Theatre around the corner. The late movie didn't get out until 9:35 which gave us thirty minutes to pull off the heist. As I shivered in the darkness waiting for the signal that everybody was in place, I wondered at the wisdom of it all. The planning had been fun but, now that the hour was at hand, I was having serious second thoughts. I didn't want to go to jail. I didn't want my family to have to come to see me and talk through those little windows while I sat on the other side in black and white stripes. I was just about to suggest that we all go back to my place for popcorn and forget the whole thing when the signal came from across the highway. It was time to go and too late to back out.

Nordie and I started for the statue prepared to remove the bolts and free the statue. Gretchen followed with the tools and a length of rope. At the same time The Mole left the depot carrying the block and tackle from his father's garage. While we were freeing the lifeless Whistle he would be attaching the block and tackle to the branch above so that we could lower the statue with ease. That left the most difficult part of the operation to Gladys and Chrome Dome. While we were carrying out our dismantling, they had to push one of the railroad carts that sat by the depot across the highway and into the park.

I took a deep breath, darted into the park and hugged the first tree I came to. I looked once behind me then I hunched over and ran for the statue at the far end. I had started on the first of the four bolts assigned to me and The Mole was already shinnying up the tree like a real Tarzan, when I realized that

Gretchen and I were alone. I listened for Nordinger but the only sound was the grating and creaking of wheels as Dome and Gladys struggled to get the cart across the highway.

"Psst! Mole. Can you see Nordie?" I was still on the first nut. We had allowed five minutes for each one and it was taking longer than that. I wouldn't have time to do Nordie's.

"No." Eddie hissed back. "The cart's half way here. Where is that dumb fuck?" Eddie said dumb fuck a lot. Eddie's father said dumb fuck a lot too, especially when he was talking to Eddie.

I could hear the crunch of metal on concrete as the cart got closer but there was no sign of Nordie. I didn't like the implications of Nordinger having disappeared. It did not bode well for the rest of the plan. I was just about to tell Gretchen to start on the other side when Nordie appeared. He was breathing hard and yelling too loud at Gretchen for his wrench.

Halvorsen's voice came out of the tree with all the force of an angry god. "What happened to you, Dumb Fuck? Get lost in the park?"

"Sorry. I had to take a pee."

"We've got thirty minutes to get all this done and you took ten minutes to pee, Nordinger. Jeez!"

"I'm sorry," Nordie whined, "It built up while I was waitin'. I couldn't help it."

"Shut up, you two." Gretched hissed. "I'll go help with the cart."

I could hear Chrome Dome cussing as they struggled to get the wheels of the cart over the curb. Gretchen's white hair bobbed up and down like a shrunken head suspended on a rubber band as they moved toward us in the dark. Nordie and I finished the bolts just as they pushed the cart in line with the back of the courageous Whistle, and Nordie secured the rope dropped by The Mole. We were just about to lift him off the pedestal when the patrol car turned on to Main Street.

The five of us on the ground dove for the darkest shadows. Except for our labored breathing, everything was quiet and normal. The patrol car seemed to move slower than usual. Perhaps the officer's sixth sense told him something was not right, because he was not only going slower he was also using his spotlight to look into buildings and dark corners on both sides of the street.

The light swept past the statue, stopped, and moved slowly back toward it again. In the brief moment the statue had been illuminated I saw the image of my own punishment. Nordie had not tied the rope under Milton's arms like he was supposed to. In his haste he had tied it around the neck of the old gentleman. When the light moved past it, I could see clearly a man hanging by his neck swinging gently back and forth while the branch above groaned out the soldier's last breath.

Gladys grabbed my arm and we waited to see if the light would swing back to the statue. When the light went out and the patrol car started to cruise toward the end of the block, I could hear the sighs of relief that came from all of us. Dome was the first one off the ground brushing the dirt from his polished head.

"O.K." he said. "We've got five minutes to get this guy loaded and out of this park."

"Maybe Nordie would like to take a pee before we get started." Eddie suggested from the tree.

"Let's quite fightin' and get this over." I was sure we would never make it before people started streaming out of the movie.

We attached the rope under Milton T's arms, raised him up and lowered him onto the cart where we laid him out flat and roped him down. The Mole undid his block and tackle and we were underway without a hitch. I was beginning to think we might get away with our little kidnapping. Even though we estimated that the statue weighed about five hundred pounds, the big wheels on the cart made it seem easy to push. Chrome Dome held the long tongue and steered while the rest of us pushed from the sides and behind. We were across the street, down the alley, and out of harm's way in no time. One of the favorite pastimes in our small town was shooting out street lights with a .22 or a slingshot or with just a rock and a good aim. There were always lights out on at least fifty percent of the corners. As luck would have it, however, we had planned a route that was lit like a ballpark. We stayed in the shadows as much as possible and tried to keep the old iron wheels from making too much noise. It was impossible, however, to make the entire seven blocks without being noticed. Several porch lights came on and we could see little slivers of light across lawns when people peeked out of their curtains. Nobody raised an alarm or inquired as to what we were doing. We might as well have been six gravediggers carting a plague-ridden corpse out of the city in the dead of night. Mrs. Dipple did report later that she had seen a small cart being pulled by a bald-headed man and a white-haired midget but she wasn't taken seriously.

We arrived at the back of the football stadium right on time. Hiding out of the lights behind the scoreboard we settled down to wait for the end of the game. Compared to getting the statue out of the park, hoisting him up to the top of the scoreboard looked like a cinch.

Nordie was taking another whiz and Chrome Dome was complaining about needing water so Gladys and I offered to go get some Cokes while we waited. It was a big game between the local high school and one of its feared rivals so the stands were packed. There was little else to do in a small town on Friday nights and the high school football games were the week's highlight. Our high school was ahead by three touchdowns at least and, with only a few minutes to play, the crowd was pretty subdued. I came up the back of the grandstands loaded down with paper cups just as the clock ran out and people started to gather up their coats and kids when Gladys grabbed my arm and sent Coke cascading over the heads of several irate adults. They were about to really lay into me when a thunderous roar went up across the field. The whole place was on its feet now and hats and arms were waving so that I had to stand on a seat to get a view of what was going on.

On the ten yard line and moving down field were the five companions we had left behind. Chrome

Dome was out in front pulling the railroad cart with black and orange streamers trailing from his neck and arms. He loped along waving to the crowd looking like he was entering the Ringling Brothers Big Top. Gretchen and Nordie, too, had found the streamers and, riding on top of the cart, they were attaching them to Milton T. Whistle as they waved and danced about the statue. The Mole brought up the rear alternately pushing the cart and blowing kisses to the crowd. Gretchen caught our eyes and waved to us to join them and by the time the cart had reached the fifty yard line Gladys and I had made our way to the field. Exhilarated by the cheers and shouts of the crowd we made a circle around the stadium bowing and waving like every good clown act does. Just as the police and school officials came running out on the field, I noticed a figure at the very top of the bleachers. There was the tiny red glow of a cigarette stuck in the corner of a broad smile. Both of his hands were made into fists with the thumbs sticking up and then the police were all around us.

The next four Saturdays of pruning, raking, and sweeping in the park passed quickly. Even the punishments given at home were barely felt. As we worked around the park, we seemed to take a great deal of pride in what we were doing and every once in awhile we would all look at one another and smile; great, genuine smiles of satisfaction.

CHAPTER XVI

*There are fish in the sea better
than have ever been caught*

I stood with my back to the wall peering over the heads of the circle of onlookers watching the dancers whirl past. The old armory hall was filled to popping. The laughter and shouts and overly loud verbal abuse of those lucky enough to find partners flew up to the high-raftered ceiling and resounded off the brick walls. The music could be heard four blocks away by those leaving the Avalon Movie Theatre and headed for Kohler's Malt Shoppe or the Dairy Freeze to get a 'softie'. I knew I had three strikes against me, at least. I ticked them off in my head as I watched Kathy Heffelman skipping past, her big "casabs," as Tom Lawson said (casabs being short for casaba melons), bouncing up and down enthusiastically to the beat of the music.

First, I thought as my head moved up and down

to the beat of Kathy's chest, I can't dance. What good were Aunt Margreg's dancing lessons. Nobody had a ballroom anymore and you sure couldn't do the waltz to "Don't Be Cruel" or "Rock of Love." Even if, by some strange chance, Lazarus and the Awakeners did play a waltz, nobody else would know how to follow me. Most of the lugs out there now could barely count to four let alone do it in rhythm. Maybe Gladys Cooper could. She was standing directly across from me crushed against the opposite wall. The blue and white checkered rims of her wing-tipped glasses stood out in the crowd like a foglight. She might just as well have been wearing World War I aviator goggles. Davey Nordinger claimed to have fogged up those glasses at the Halloween party. Nobody contested the assertion. Nobody cared.

The music slopped to an enthusiastic ending and everyone applauded with their mouths. Great articulate stuff like, "dig it daddy-o" and "bitchin 7" and "crazy man crazy". The greasers, of course, remained cool and detached, their thumbs in the back pockets of their jeans keeping them just off the hip so that the crack in their butts showed through the white T shirts. Which brought to mind the second strike against me. I was big on baseball terms. I was a baseball nut. It was about the only thing I could do besides walk that didn't cause me some kind of embarrassment. If I were to walk out there in search of some willing sacrificial virgin, the greaser lugs would rip me apart just on the grounds of the outfit I was wearing. My mother had insisted that I wear my new maroon cords with a pink shirt. She thought I looked real dashing and "neat." When she said neat, of course, she meant clean and well pressed but I let it go without comment. She meant well. Whenever she bought me new clothes she always insisted that they were "the latest thing." I never pinned her down as to how she determined this fashion statement but they couldn't afford a lot and she did her best. Once she bought me a pair of knickers and said, "They're coming back in." She had insisted I wear them to school with a yellow checked sweater vest and a purple shirt. That bit of fashion cost me a bloody nose and a dunk in the school incinerator at the hands of Butch Keller. The worst thing about getting beat up by Butch was that he always pinned your shoulders down with his knees to give you the old "scalp burn" and he smelled like two-day-old piss. He probably only had one pair of underwear. At least, I thought, my mom gives me clean shorts and I don't smell like a bedpan. Still, I couldn't walk right out in the middle of those guys in the zoot suit I was wearing and expect to come out unscathed.

The final strike against me was the most insurmountable, at least in my own mind. I had always been a scrawny kid. So much so, in fact, that in high school my nickname became "P.F.". It started the day I went to work on a ranch bucking bales of hay. I was introduced to the boss and he about knocked himself out laughing.

"Kind of a puny fucker ain't he?" He followed that with a slap on the back that almost knocked me over and then walked away buckled over with laughter. Nobody dared call me puny fucker around the boss's wife so I became known simply as "P.F.". All things considered, my chances of getting the girl I wanted were slim to none.

Lazarus and the Awakeners announced they would be taking a short break, which resulted in equal amounts of boos, catcalls, and cheers. I would be able to move about the floor now without fear of my "outfit" being noticed. I had been fantasizing all afternoon about asking Mary Jo Halverson to dance. In my mind, we would see each other across a crowded room, lock eyes, and, with breath coming from deep within our mutually aroused loins, we would weave untouched by the milling masses to the center of the room, glide easily into each others' arms, and begin to bend sensuously to the music. The song was clear in my mind as well. I hummed softly to myself as I searched the room for her nut brown hair.

In my head I sounded exactly like Sam Cook and my confidence grew as I sought out the reality of my dreams. Suddenly I saw her standing at the foot of the stage, her head twisted backward so that her hair fell off her shoulder and her profile was caught in the amber light. I could feel her warm laughter flow out to me as I fumbled my way toward her. God, she's great, I thought. What a face, what a body, what... I couldn't call them casabs. That would be too vulgar for my image of Mary Jo. They were more like...what? More like puppies, I thought. That was it! Small, soft puppies nesting beneath her blouse. Wow, yes! That was it! Little chihuahuas snuggling there, waiting, waiting for me to.....Chi Hua Hua.

"Hi, Jackie." I turned reluctantly away from my

canine image to see Gladys grinning with all the flashing, orthodontic brilliance of a tinsel factory.

"Oh, hi Cooper. How's it goin'?"

"Wonderful, Jackie. I'm having a wonderful time. Isn't this the loveliest?"

Gladys had taken to ending her sentences with a stupid superlative of some kind. Like, isn't Sister Clara Williams the smartest? Or, your shirt is the keenest. I was sure she thought it made her sound cool but she succeeded in just sounding stupid and out of it. But, she was nice enough and she always looked like she might shed big crocodile tears if you so much as said boo to her. Consequently, it was tough to be mean to Gladys Cooper. I just kind of avoided saying much for fear I might be the one to open the dike and drown the whole world.

"Have you been dancing a lot, Jackie? I mean, the music is the coolest.   What did you mean by chihuahua? Have you got a dog, Jackie? I mean a puppy? Puppies are the cuddliest."

Realizing I must have said chihuahua out loud, I was more than a little flustered. Besides, Gladys had this patronizing grin on her face like she was baiting me.

"Ya. I mean...I haven't got a dog. Well, I do, a black lab. I mean I don't have a chihuahua, Cooper, but I imagine they are very cuddly. How about you? Been dancin'?"

I looked over at the stage just in time to see Mary Jo take some guy's hand and move off into the crowd. Damn, I thought, that was Butch. Damn Butch Keller, the lug, and damn Gladys Cooper. Why did she have to pick on me right in the middle of a fantasy come true.

"I like your outfit, Jackie. It's the neatest."

"Ya, well, thanks. Look, I was just gonna meet some of the guys outside for a fag. I should get goin'"

Gladys just stood there. Women never make it easy. They always just stand there or just look at you or something that makes a guy feel like a big louse. I wondered why she wore those goofy glasses all the time. They made her eyes look a thousand times too big. Tears rushing out of those eyes would leave puddles at your feet and everybody in the place would know you were the schmuck that hurt nice Gladys Cooper. I felt compelled to cover my tracks.

"Listen, how about a dance later? A nice slow one. We'll wow 'em with our foot work." I started off before she could find something else to say.

"That would be the nicest," she said to my back. "It wouldn't make my night but it would be nice." I turned to look at her but she had already turned around and was moving into the crowd.

"How did they do it?" I wondered out loud. They must sneak off and take special classes for girls on how to make guys feel like worms.

I pushed my way out the side door and stepped out onto the narrow loading dock that, on Friday nights, billowed clouds of smoke out of the alley like a living organism. I bummed a Pall Mall from Gordy Masters and looked around for Butch. I knew Butch would be cupping a fag in his hand looking cool and "debonair" and he would be standing somewhere obvious. Butch liked to be noticed. He was of the impression that he was born to lead the squalid masses. Butch was a lug but at the moment Mary Jo was on his arm and I wanted to find them. Why I would think about punishing myself in this way I don't know but the pull of Mary Jo's chihuahuas was strong and I was willing to suffer whatever humiliation was necessary just to get close to them. At thirteen, I hadn't had a lot of experience. Well. O.K., I hadn't had any. But in my heart and in my mind I had lived a thousand thrilling moments. Moments that gave me a sense of what "being with" Mary Jo might bring to reality. I dropped the butt of my fag and ground it out with a saddle-shoed toe. The band would be returning soon for their last set. Time was running out. Tom Lawson always said, "If you don't make your move by ten o'clock you either scrape something off the bottom of the barrel or whack off when you get home." This bit of advanced wisdom had been shortened by most to "scrape it or whack it." I had never done either but I was getting desperate. Melvin Hobson had told me once that "Ya just had to do it because if ya didn't a huge pressure would build up in your scrotum and, given too much time, yer balls would burst." I had no intention of letting that happen. If my balls blew up it wasn't going to happen too awfully far from Mary Jo Halverson.

I had just about given up when I saw them coming down the alley from the street. Butch had his arm draped over her shoulder and his pudgy little lug face was pushed into her hair. Mary Jo was laughing as she put her arm around his waist and leaned into him. I was sure I could see the foam dripping from his lecherous lips. He looked up to the crowd with his usual toothy grin and I thought, for crying out loud, he has been salivating right in her ear and she loves it. I could never get away with that. I had blown in Kathy Heffelman's ear once at the school square dance, on Lawson's suggestion, of course. Lawson said they went wild for that kind of thing but all I got for my effort was a size thirteen foot smashed down on my instep. Of course, Kathy was an animal of a different stripe. She was a good foot and one half taller than I and I had to get up quite a wind to reach her ear. I suppose now that the effect was somewhat less than sexually stimulating. Still, it galled me that guys like Butch could get away with crap like that. It really galled me. As Butch and Mary Jo stepped up to the platform I found myself face to face with the loving couple.

"Hey, Laney, cool. I dig that outfit. Your old lady got it for ya right?" He turned to Mary Jo. "Laney's gonna start dressin' himself real soon. Ain't ya, Laney?" They both had a good laugh and pushed past me to go into the hall. I have no idea what got into me. It must have had something to do with protecting my mother. A guy could take all kinds of crap but it wasn't right to say things against a guy's mother. Mothers were sacrosanct or something and Butch had crossed the line. My skinny, little arm reached out of its own accord and grasped the white t shirt pulling it free from Butch's jeans. That thin layer of shirt must have been all that held the jeans up because as soon as it was pulled free Butch's pants fell to his knees revealing the stained jockey shorts of the town tough.

Had it happened in the school yard it would have been bad enough, but here in front of the entire town, in front of Mary Jo, there was no question.

I was as good as dead. Butch yanked on his jeans, stuffed in his shirt, and stood facing the crowd which had dissolved into laughter. Every faction of every gang in town was rolling on the ground practically beating their heads against the walls at Butch's expense. My respect for Butch Keller grew in that moment. He might be a lug and a "puppy-napper" as well, but he straightened himself up and looked straight into the eye of every single one of those laughing hyenas. When the laughter had died completely he turned to face me.

"It was an accident," I stammered, "Honest, I just wanted to get your attention. I didn't know...you know...I didn't..."

I didn't know what I had intended really. To protect my mother? Maybe. To protect my name? Maybe. Certainly not to protect my right to wear maroon pants. I hated them a lot more than Butch Keller did. To impress Mary Jo? How did I expect to do that by picking a fight with the toughest guy in town? I had just done it and now Mary Jo was laughing at me because she knew what was coming as well as I did. Butch was laughing at me too but there seemed to be something else in his eyes. It wasn't hate or even anger. It looked a lot like sympathy but that didn't make sense.

I had a flash of another time when I had seen that same look. I don't remember what my infraction had been but it resulted in my father walking ahead of me toward the barn slowly removing his heavy belt from his trousers. When he turned to face me I could see in his eyes that he didn't want to strike me. Apparently I had put my father in an impossible situation. The licking I got was not severe. The real hurt came from seeing the look in my father's eyes. I stood very still knowing what Butch had to do. The crowd backed away and was quiet. After all, they had all seen Rebel Without a Cause and Blackboard Jungle. They knew how to behave in order to achieve maximum effect.

They want to see me bleed, I thought. Well, up theirs! I wasn't going to grovel and I wasn't going to cower like a puppy. Oh my God, I thought, a puppy. The chihuahuas are gone forever.

At that moment Butch's hand snaked out from his side and snapped into my nose. Before I could react to the pain, his left hand hit me somewhere on the head and then I felt a terrific pain in my right eye and my knees buckled. I tried to remain standing. I tried to hold on to some kind of dignity but the effort was lost and I crumbled to the ground.

I knew I hadn't passed out completely. I was aware of the crowd moving back into the hall grumbling that the fight was too short and that there was too little blood. I was thinking vaguely that the music had started again and then she was there. She was bending over me. She hadn't turned away with the others. She hadn't really laughed at me then. Here she was holding my head and dabbing at my nose with a small, sweet smelling hanky. Oh God, the pain was worth it. The fantasy come true. She would tend to me, heal me, take care of me. Butch Keller, my mind screamed, "I love your ass!"

"That's a strange sentiment," Gladys said, "considering he has just turned your face into a squashed plum." Out of one blurry eye I saw the checkered glasses and let my head roll back into her arms.

"Don't attempt to put the eye back in, Gladys. Just call the ambulance. It will be a delicate operation. Maybe I'll get partial sight back, who knows."

"Don't be such a baby, Jackie. You have a bloody nose and you will probably have a big black eye tomorrow, but the ambulance won't be necessary."

"Ya? You don't think so, hah? Sure as hell feels like it." I looked up at her. "What happened to things like, 'your face is the nastiest' or 'the fight was the keenest'? You're losing your cool, Cooper."

She laughed. It was a nice laugh, full and unrestrained. It was the realest.

The bleeding had stopped and the short walk to Kohler's had cleared some of the dizziness but I was still not feeling all that stable. The hot chocolate malt we were sharing, however, was bringing me around and I ventured a look at Gladys sitting across from me.

"Don't stare at me, Jackie. It makes me uncomfortable."

"Sorry. How come you wear those glasses, Cooper? Can you see without 'em?"

She turned bright red and stared at the straw melting in the chocolate malt.

"No.   I can't see a thing without them."   She laughed. "Don't you like my glasses, Laney?"

"Oh, sure.   They're fine.   You know, glasses are glasses. I mean, they're just fine, sure."

"No, you don't like them I can tell.   I don't like them much either.   As a matter of fact, I hate them. But my mother picked them out.   She thinks they're great."

"Ya! I can dig that.   I understand completely. Really!   According to her they're the latest thing, right?"

"The latest." She mimicked.   We both laughed then as we looked closely at each other.   Then we went at the malt with new vigor. After we had slurped loudly at the bottom and around the edges, we leaned back and looked self-consciously down at our hands.

I was confused as usual. What was it? Did guys always respond to the Florence Nightingale who tended their wounds or was I, as Tom Lawson put it, scraping it?

"So, what do ya think, Cooper? Want me to walk ya home?"

"Maybe I should walk you home.   You don't look too good, Jackie."

"Naw. I'm fine.   You're on my way.   I could drop you off and head on home."

"Well, O.K. if you want to. But you don't have to. I mean, you don't owe me anything or anything. You know?"   She stopped and leaned across the table. "You don't have to feel like you have to walk me home. I can call. I usually do."

"No, I want to.   I'd like to, Gladys, if that'd be

O.K."

As we stepped out of the Malt Shoppe I could hear Lazarus and the Awakeners doing a rendition of "Unchained Melody." Lazarus' voice was a poor substitution for Sam Cook and I started to sing the lyrics.

The streetlights, the ones still lit, filtered through the trees and splashed a pattern of light onto the pavement. Between the lights was a gentle darkness that made the night quiet and comfortable. Perhaps because it hid the color in her cheeks, Gladys picked one of these spots to speak.

"I don't have chihuahuas, Jackie." I wasn't quite sure I had heard her right, or maybe I was afraid I had.

"What?"

"I said, I don't have chihuahuas."

There was a long silence. In the vague light at the corner I turned toward her.

"How did you know?"

Gladys shrugged. "After you fell and the others left I came over to help you. I love blood you know?"

"Ya, I bet."

"Well you were kind of foggy and out of it and you thought I was...her. I mean Mary Jo, I guess and were...or thought you were....ah caressing her ummm...chihuahuas I think you said, no, actually you moaned."

"I moaned?"

"Ah ha, you moaned."

"Did I actually..you know, did I caress...?"

"No. Oh, no I moved back a little."

"Just a little, Huh?"

"I told you, I don't have chihuahuas." We had started to walk again and had reached another stretch of darkness. "More like hushpuppies, I'd say."

"Hushpuppies? What is a hushpuppy?" She hesitated like she was trying to make the image fit. "Kind of a small potato patty only cornmeal I think."

"Hushpuppy, huh? I don't know if I could get into that."

"I don't think anybody invited you to, Jackie."

"No. Well, no I didn't mean that. I just...ya know. Well I do look pretty pathetic don't you think. You know, injured and..."

"I think you'll live. But keep trying you'll find someone who might fall for that sympathy thing. Well, here we are. I would stand here and wait to see if you would kiss me but I am not sure if you did you would be thinking of me".

With that she turned and opened the door.

"Thanks for walking me home. It was the coolest"

~ ~ ~ ~

I stood there under her porch light for several minutes before I turned to go. On the very slow walk to my house I concentrated on kicking a small stone out in front of me and every time I nudged it a little closer to my back porch I couldn't help thinking that once again I had missed something, something I might never get back.

CHAPTER XVII

God prefers prayers to tears

It was not the kind of day Bridget Laney would have wished for. My Great Aunt Bridey was not a dreary person. I preferred to see her as a person who not only lived, but dreamed in the sunshine. A person of summer flowers and warm, gentle breezes and close evenings full of morning glory and candescent sky. Yet, the day did have an appropriate kind of charm. A "soft" day, the Irish would say, complete with weeping sky and gossamer mist. The damp chill hunched the shoulders and touched the bones of those who stood about. They seemed content with the weather, able to join with it and, so, feel more comfortable in their somberness. And, too, Bridget was beyond caring about this day or any other future day. She had no need now for even the memory of sunshine or flowers or fading pictures glued to black and dusty pages. Those faithless, transient, and corporal illusions were left to those of us who still lived and needed them. So, I didn't begrudge the weather either except that my feet were cold and I couldn't concentrate properly on being sad. I wanted very much to be sad. I wanted to remember this day as the saddest of all days but the cold and the wet and the image of Aunt Bridey's twinkling eyes as deep as a midnight sky kept intruding on my grief. I shifted back and forth on my feet and tried to listen to the inspiring words of Father Shea but my thoughts kept wandering. We were facing toward the blackberry hedge looking, the way Aunt Bridey would be looking now, out across the fallow fields and the coming winter sky. I remembered a time about a million years ago when I had sat in the warmth of a summer night and tried to play a silver flute. I could still feel that silver flute and I could still feel Lynn beneath my hand. I found myself searching the crowd to see if she was there. I didn't want to forget her. I was suddenly frightened that I would forget everything about this place and about those who stood like shadows around the grave. I would never forget Aunt Bridey, I thought. I would never forget Aunt Margreg or Aunt Jane. I would remember everything about the farm and the land. But even then the images were fading. The people and events overshadowed the growing importance of my new life.

The slight drizzle was turning into a steady downpour as the late November sky opened up. An icy wind picked up and slanted the rain making umbrellas useless. Father Shea finished his comments in a rush and people made a mad dash for their cars. When I looked back, there was nothing to indicate that we had just put Aunt Bridey in the ground. There was only a cemetery cast, without detail, against a leaded background. As our family started to make our way back to the waiting cars, I saw her standing by her parents and her brother Robert. She stepped toward me but her mother caught her hand and held her back. She didn't wave like she had at the crossroads the day we left the farm, but her eyes held mine and she smiled. I knew I would not forget everything or everyone. Some things would never fade.

The wake had been held for several days before the funeral with people dropping in at all hours to eat and drink and pass by the coffin, which stood open in the parlor. More people had come for the funeral and now they would all be stopping by the house again to visit and add to the vast quantities of food that already filled every room in the house.

My mother insisted that I stay visible to greet people and to help carry away coats and hats and dripping umbrellas. The soft murmurings filled with condolences, offers of help, and "I remember whens" drifted through the rooms with the constant motion of the guests. There was occasional quiet laughter and the ring of plates and silver as food was prepared and set out. It all became a dizzying whirl that I could not escape. I was simply part of the blur letting myself be carried from place to place, from conversation to conversation by the movement of others. Finally I was able to find an opening in the fluid crowd and I slipped outside on to the porch.

The wind bent the trees and the meadow grass and pushed the rain under the overhanging roof so that I had to stand against the wall to keep from getting wet. I had just taken a deep breath welcoming the quiet and the cool air when I saw my Aunt Mary. She was standing at the end of the porch, her hands resting on the railing, as she looked out into the rain. I thought of my aunt as perpetually in a housedress and an apron, her hair fixed hurriedly and never quite in place. The lady in a fashionable black dress, hair done up in a bun and held in place with a black velvet ribbon, was a different picture altogether. She stood with her back straight against the wind and let the rain wash over her face and dampen her clothes so that they clung to her body. I watched for a few moments afraid of disturbing her yet fearful that something was wrong.

"Aunt Mary, Is everything all right?" I felt I had to speak in case she needed something, but she didn't seem to hear me. The rain jumped off the porch roof and was driven against the immobile woman in sheets so that I knew she must have been soaked to the skin. Yet she continued to face into the weather like a determined sea captain. I wondered what might have her so preoccupied that she would stand there so oblivious. I didn't know then that she stood rigid against the wind and the rain because she wanted to feel them both wash over her, that she was acutely aware of the sensation and that it reminded her of another rain in another place a very long time ago.

~~~~~

Young Mary Shields had been carefully planning for the Box Social for months. The delicacies, founded in old family recipes, were packed with care and tied up with fancy ribbon sure to catch the eye of every young man at the Social. Mary had stood in front of her mirror and been quite pleased, too, with what she saw. The new dress, her very first store bought, was just the right color for a dark haired girl on a sunny day. The ribbon in her hair matched both the dress and the tie on her lunch box.

Now she stood on tiptoe looking among the crowd for the one she hoped would bid the highest when her box was auctioned off. She knew every boy in town, of course, and most every boy in the county, but there was just one that she wanted to see. The bidding had already started on Sally Hutche's basket and Patty Meiker's had been sold for a lot more than Mary thought it was worth. She hoped he wouldn't be late. She had cooked and baked especially to please him and he would have to be a complete ninny not to notice that the ribbons matched, so he was sure to bid on the right lunch.

When her box was raised high above the auctioneer's head and the first bid was made, her heart sank. She couldn't see him anywhere. In fact, there was no sign of any of the boys from Kilkerry. Suppose he didn't show up at all or came too late to bid on her special lunch. She would have to spend the afternoon with some stranger or, even worse, a lecherous old widower looking for a young wife to service his needs.   The bidding had reached two dollars and she knew it wouldn't go much beyond that. If he didn't materialize soon, she was doomed.

"Two dollars," the auctioneer called. "Do I hear three?   Three dollars for this lovely lunch packed with.."   Here he paused to sniff carefully around the corners of the box. "Do I smell rhubarb pie?   Come gentlemen. Who will bid three dollars?"

"Two fifty!"   Came the bid from the back of the crowd.   But it wasn't Seamus's voice, she could tell. He had promised he would come in time.   She squeezed her eyes tight and wished and wished with all her might.

"I have two fifty.   Two fifty.   Do I hear two seventy five.   Two seventy five.   Two fifty going once..."

"Three"

"Three dollars. Thank you sir. Three dollars and what am I bid.   Three dollars then going, going, and....."

"And two bits."   Mary opened her eyes and saw him standing on a bench way in the back and waving his hat over his head of curly hair so the auctioneer wouldn't miss him.

They took their lunch to the top of Hutche's hill, spread the blanket out in the sunniest spot away from all the trees and the other couples.   Seamus Laney placed his sweat-stained hat on his knee, raved about the rhubarb pie and asked Mary Shields if she would consent to be his wife.

The rain came suddenly sending most of the picnickers running for cover.   The couples grabbed blankets and picnic baskets and dashed for the cover of the gazebo or into the parish hall where they could finish their meal and wait out the storm. The rain did not dampen the spirits of those who had too few occasions to mix and to be social. The courting would go on between the younger couples, and the older folks would not give up the opportunity to gossip at length and to talk about the crops and the latest political blunders. Only two remained on the hillside oblivious to the rain. Like all young couples, they talked of the future. They dared, perhaps for the very first time, to speak of their dreams and, together, they laid the plans that would make those dreams come true. And all the while the rain ran down their shining faces like tears of joy. Their clothes clung to them and they clung to each other and Mary thought she had never been so happy. When they finally began to shiver, they reluctantly walked down the hill, faces raised to the sky, their hands entwined against all the unseen forces that might threaten them.

She couldn't have guessed then how strong that grip would have to be if she were to stay by her husband's side and face a future that waited in a tall white house built by her husband's father. The Judge had never held hands in the rain or, if he had, it was long ago and lost to the years. He did know that his son was marrying an outsider and he was not pleased. When she first came up the long drive with her young husband she thought she had never seen anything so grand as that house. The wide veranda shaded by lilacs, afforded a view of the meadows and the setting sun that cast a pastel glow over the world that would fulfill the dreams expressed on Hutche's hill. The secret she held close to her heart through all the years of growing children, nursing her sisters-in-law, and looking after that fancy house was cast on that very first visit. She knew that some day that house would be hers. Some day she would no longer be the outsider but, instead, the mistress of the house that stood on the hill.

Some day she would finish her cleaning and washing and cooking and she would step out on to her veranda and watch the rain bring evening, clean and fresh outside her door. That secret, pressed like a precious stone in the palm of her hand, kept her from despair. It allowed her to hum softly as she worked and kept her, too, from bending her shoulders beneath the weight of responsibility and the chill of a narrow-minded family. She waited patiently for her time to come.

Mary stood almost as tall as my Uncle Shay and, often, when they entwined their fingers and walked the mile or so down the road to their own home she would rest her head against his and they would both be reminded of their dreams. Dreams that were somehow swallowed in a whirlpool of duty and the business of living day to day. Thoughts of baseball fame gave way to the drudgery of working the farm and visions of picnics on sun-washed hillsides faded with the tedium of putting food on the table. Still, a small secret kept Mary warm and she would grasp her husband's hand a bit tighter as she glanced over her shoulder to her house on the hill.

~ ~ ~ ~

"Aunt Mary?" I said again, raising my voice over the wind and the rain. She turned, her thoughts still glazing her eyes.

"Jackie. I didn't hear you come out. Is everything alright?"

"I was worried that you were getting wet. You might catch cold, Aunt Mary."

"Oh, I'm not cold, Jackie." She reached out wanting me to take her hand. "Come here, Jackie. Can you see how fast the clouds are moving across the sky? And feel how warm the rain is." The rain was not warm at all. But I looked up at the clouds and nodded as she put her arm around me and hugged me close.

"Will you miss Aunt Bridey much, Aunt Mary?"

It took her a long time to speak and when she finally did I wasn't quite sure she had really given me the answer. "It was Bridget's time." she said. "Everything on God's earth has its time." She hugged me tighter and smiled down at me. "All good farm boys know that, Jackie. There is a time to reap and a time to sow. A time to harvest and a time to plant. Only those who don't understand that have a need to be sad."

"Aunt Margreg and Aunt Jane will be lonely though without Aunt Bridey. They'll be sad, won't they?"

"Your Aunt Jane and Aunt Margreg have been lonely for a long, long time but, no, I don't think they will be sad, Jackie. They understand about time. Perhaps they understand it far better than the rest of us."

We stood there, letting the rain flatten our hair and soak through our clothes, until I felt her shiver next to me. "Well, I suppose you are right, Jackie. We shouldn't stand here and catch our death. Let's see if we can't find you a cup of hot cocoa and a slice of pie."

She took my hand and we stepped out of the rain and entered the long hallway. She was smiling slightly perhaps knowing that my Aunt Margreg would soon follow her sister and that Aunt Jane, the oldest, would have a difficult time in the empty parlor all alone. It was only a question of time and Aunt Mary would have the house she had lived and worked for. When I look back and see her again standing in the November rain, I wonder if she didn't also know that by the time that happened, the old house would hardly be worth having. Her children would be all grown and gone, the husband who had waved his hat so high above the crowd would let his fingers slip from hers too soon. The flood of circumstance and the erosion of too many years would give her the house too late. Everything has its time.

CHAPTER XVIII

*The schoolhouse bell sounds bitter in youth
but sweet in old age*

Bobby Settlemeyer pitched side arm, chewed Bazooka bubble gum and wore his pants too low. The combined moves on the mound were mysterious and wonderful to watch. The stretch went up, the gum shifted from right to left, the pants dropped slightly and then the process reversed itself. His right hand fell back and whipped across the front of his body, the gum slid over to the right again, and the pants regained a tenuous hold on his hips. More often than not the boy at bat was unable to deal with either the unfamiliar side arm of the pitcher or the apparent way in which his pants defied the law of gravity. As a result, Settlemeyer became one of the most feared pitchers in the Knights of Columbus League and a near legend in his own time. Of course, with the pitcher's rise to fame the rest of the team was able to bask in the backwash of his glory. We saw ourselves as the "well-oiled machine." We whipped the ol' apple around the horn after each out with professional zeal and practiced aplomb and chattered constantly in the accepted lingo. Some sixth sense told us that these two functions of the ballplayer, carried out in the proper manner, not only intimidated the other team but directly affected the outcome of the game.

Our infield was an awesome power, enclosing the batter in what we pictured as an impenetrable net. Kelly LaGrand played shortstop in the tradition of Pee Wee Reese. No taller than the average drinking fountain, he was speckled with freckles each one separate from the other never running to blotches and matched by nature in color to the thick growth of hair. All of which gained him the unoriginal moniker of 'Sandy.' The fielder's mitt attached to his arm looked large enough to scoop up footballs. He would crouch like a Cheshire Ape midway between second and third skimming the great glove along the dirt as he swung it from left to right encouraging the fearsome Settlemeyer with a stream of "Chuck 'er in there, chuck 'er in there. Hum babe, hum babe. Ha now, ha now chuck 'er in there, Bobby babe."

On Sandy's right, deep in the third base position, was Davey Nordinger. Davey fell short of being menacing but not from lack of effort. Hunched slightly at the shoulders, he leveled a totally unintelligible series of insulting vowels at the batter, the ump, and the entire opposing bench while scratching his cleats in the dirt like a challenged bull in the arena. A quarter bushel of Durham wheat sprung from under his ball cap nearly pushing it off of his head. However, the cherubic face that could never quite find a grimace kept him from striking total fear in the hearts of our opponents.   The entire league was aware that even though he stood on the outfield grass line, Davey could fire the ball to first base, not in the usual grade school arc, but in a perfectly straight line that ended with a beautiful whack in the web of the first baseman's mitt. Our coach allowed Davey to play this far back because of his tremendous arm and only those of us who had played Pee Wee ball with 'Nordie' knew the truth about that deep position. In fifth grade the then newly appointed third baseman, had rushed to scoop up a hard hit grounder only to find himself doubled over on his back moaning in agony while the coach pedaled his legs in an effort to relieve the pain that threatened his puberty.   This questionable emergency treatment, we all knew , was designed to let everyone in the stands, especially the girls, know exactly what had happened and where boys were most vulnerable.   Davey was convinced that the attention given to his injury was calculated to embarrass him to the extent that he would never again allow such a thing to happen.   From that time on he took up a position some five feet behind the bag and would not be budged.

Unlike the stern and vociferous Davey Nordinger, Tom Lawson danced about first base grinning from one Dumbo ear to the other in a constant display of good sportsmanship.   He joked with the runners and demonstrated his unique ability to eject long streams of saliva through the space in his front teeth with the accuracy of a Buck Rogers laser beam. This talent was not totally wasted on Mary Jo Halverson, who hopped up and down on the sidelines, a brown-eyed Kangaroo Rat with swishing pom poms. The endless supply of spit could be aimed to within a millimeter of the runner's foot. The irritated target would unconsciously inch further and further away from the bag to avoid the disgusting discharge until the uncanny Bobby Settlemeyer would drop his left foot and, with pants hovering dangerously low, pick off the unsuspecting victim. To add to this humiliation, Lawson would cluck his tongue and slap the runner on the butt as he sheepishly retreated to the bench.

Eddie "The Mole" was the professional second baseman and captain of our team. He constantly threw blades of grass in the air to check the wind, dusted his toes on his stockinged calf and watched each instant of play collecting statistics as coupons to be cashed in later. The Mole was privy to the secret knowledge that he could cover the entire infield by himself if the need ever arose. In fact, he often made up elaborate stories during practice that gradually eliminated the rest of the players leaving only himself in the final game of the World Series dashing from position to position astounding the cheering crowd of thousands with his dexterity and precision.

Lost in the background of these red and white jerseyed heroes, covered with chest pad, face mask, and cap turned bill backward, I hunkered down behind home plate and assessed our chances. Nobody was particularly concerned about whether we won or lost the first game of the season. The coach was not concerned about the win-loss record at all. In fact, he preferred a few loses at the beginning of the season to keep the young egos in line. The fans simply wanted to see a ball game and the players were just working out the winter kinks and warming to the sense of Spring. Still, nobody really liked to lose quite as badly as we were at that point in the game. Being down six to zero in the top of the eighth is nobody's idea of a good time and, to the thirteen-year-old, is nothing short of the end of the world, at least until Dairy Queen has provided the antidote.

Nordie had experienced another near miss to the crotch in the top of the fifth and had retreated halfway into the outfield in the hope of making it through puberty the same gender as he went in. Sandy had shoveled up a blistering grounder on his way to a double play that could have saved three runs, only to rifle a handful of dirt to the disgusted Mole on second. To top it off, Bobby was allowing too many hits into our bungling outfield. Tom Lawson had risen to a height of jocularity that disgusted everyone but the pom pom girls while I tried desperately, as one-half of the battery, to keep the 'well-oiled machine' running. It wasn't so much that I wanted to win. Winning always provided only a momentary euphoria that passed quickly. What I wanted, but would never have admitted even to myself, was a chance to stand out as a part of the team. Oh, a catcher had moments I suppose. Moving the outfield from left to right, shallow or deep. Adjusting the infield. Flashing a few signals to a pitcher who could only throw one kind of pitch and an occasional run to the backstop in an attempt to catch a popup foul. The real moments of glory, however, were reserved for the rest of the team. Fans noticed the spectacular handling of a hard hit ball, the precision of a double play. They stood and cheered in recognition of an outfielder backed against the fence, reaching into the blue afternoon and plucking a home run off of the stat sheets. Even playing my very best, I went unnoticed. I had always felt that the coach saw me and the ball bag in much the same way. We were both taken along as important accouterments used during the game and stuffed into the back of the station wagon when it was all over. My hope lay, not in saving the team from defeat, but rather, in that the next inning and one half would provide me with a chance to make the singular play that would astound everyone, most especially Mary Jo Halverson.

Since fourth grade I had watched from the back of the crowd, my teammates slapped on the back, hugged, and lifted triumphantly onto their fellow's shoulders. I had watched, too, the gleeful attention given to such heroes by Mary Jo and the other cheerleaders.

As I dug Seddlemeyer's first pitch of the inning out of the dirt, I knew that if the play came now, early in the season, I could capture at once the admiration of my teammates, the respect of my coach, and the attention of Mary Jo. This could last, I suspected, for several games, perhaps even the entire season if it were truly an unforgettable play. She would tremble with excitement and the unattainable would be mine. Whoever put forth the axiom that boys my age were more interested in their baseballs, model planes, and bicycles than they were in the opposite sex must have lived their early life in a foot locker.   The pubescent transition may be awkward and confusing but it comes with devastating speed and even before its unfailing arrival the seeds of preparation are planted. I am sure I had no idea what I would do with Mary Jo's lavish attention but something in my genes told me it would be a magnificent discovery.

My chances slipped away a little further as the first man in the lineup went down swinging. Seddlemeyer worked the second one to a full count and then allowed a popup that The Mole handled with ease.   The third batter grounded out to short and we ended the inning one, two, three. My batting average was in the low two hundreds and, while I managed to avoid many disgraces at bat, I never sent them out of the park either.   All I could do was wait and hope for the big play in the top of the ninth.

Our center fielder, Joey Pentellio, looked like he ate pasta three meals a day and snacked on cold pizza. This high caloric diet pushed Joey out but not up which resulted in giving the opposing pitcher a strike zone six inches high.   It was no surprise that Joey was walked more than anyone else in the league. In the bottom of the eighth, however, Joey powered one deep into right field. Even with a huge heap of lunchtime rigatoni holding him back he made a standup double. He stood on second base like he was king of the mountain and waved jubilantly to Mrs. Pentellio as everyone cheered.   A single by the right fielder gave us men on first and third and we were at the top of our order. We had managed to fill the bases with only one out by the time The Mole stepped up to bat cleanup. I was on deck knocking the nonexistent dirt out of my cleats watching Eddy glare at the rattled pitcher. Joey Pentellio was taking a big lead off third with visions of lasagna dancing in his head.

"Better move yer outfield, pitch. The Mole's gonna send her out of the park," he yelled. Sure enough Eddie took the first pitch and before it even cleared the infield everyone was on their feet and Joey was rolling over home plate. It was four to six and I was up. I had visions of Eddie walking hand in hand with Mary Jo Halverson and the ump called strike one. I had visions of Mary Jo Halverson laughing at me and the ump called strike two. I had visions of Mary Jo Halverson having malted milks with Joey Pentellio and I was out. Out at bat, out of luck, and out in the cold. We went into the top of the ninth down two runs and I had three outs to make the play that would win me fame and lasting love.

By the time the first batter had struck out I was cursing Bobby Seddlemeyer and willing his pants down around his ankles. How could I make a play if nobody hit the ball. The second batter had gotten to first on an error and then it happened. A gift from the great baseball player in the sky; my dream come true. Mary Jo Halverson was mine, the entire cheerleading squad was mine. The man on first was taking a big lead off the bag and his first base coach was touching himself all over his body. I knew the runner had the signal and was going on the next pitch. I flashed my thumb to the right between my legs and Seddlemeyer nodded.

The pitch came high and to the outside. The batter reached across and swung. A foul tip off the end of his bat. I was moving already and dove for the ball that miraculously got snagged in the web of my glove. Blinded by dirt and throwing from a prone position, I rifled the ball to first and nailed the runner before he could make his outstretched fingers touch the bag. It was a double play, a spectacular double play from home plate. I had saved the inning and we had one more chance to bring in two runs and tie the game. The team bounded off the field and surrounded me with cheers and swats on the butt. I could see Mary Jo hopping up and down and waving her pom poms in my direction. The coach pumped my hand and ushered me to the bench with a shower of compliments. Joy was mine! I had become one of the heroes. I was part of the well-oiled machine.

I was still radiating by the coach's side when I heard the crack. There was no mistaking that sound. While I planned my future pleasures and grinned at Mary Jo, we had put two men on and now Sandy had plastered a homer and we had won the first game of the season. The team was lining up at home and shaking the hands of each runner as they trotted across the plate. When Sandy came in he was lifted to the shoulders of Davey Nordinger and Tom Lawson and the cheerleaders were doing a primitive victory dance around the threesome. I stood once again at the edge of the crowd and watched as Mary Jo reached up and with promise in her smile took the hand of Kelly.

My father put his arm around my shoulder and as we followed Kelly and his entourage out of the park, he stopped and turned us around to face the diamond. "I always loved playing the game of baseball," he said. "Looking at that empty field I can conjure up some great memories. What about you?"

He was way ahead of me, of course. I was still in the process of making memories and the one I had mapped out for myself had just turned into a great one for someone else. It wasn't that I hated Kelly for very long. I just hated him at that moment, and through the night, and into the next day. Late into the next day.

CHAPTER XVIIII

Unwillingness easily finds an excuse

Having moved away from the farm, its simplicity and its rustic age-old routines, my family slipped into their new life. Some of the changes came easily, even unnoticed and some faced serious resistance. My father had always worked in the city and his transition was, perhaps, the easiest. He moved easily and naturally into suburban life happy to return to the farm only for the occasional visit and fall hunting season. Holding on only to his usual farm breakfast, now supplemented by mid-morning coffee and donuts, until his death in 1985. My sister embraced her new school and new friends barely skipping a beat. My mother, perhaps because she never truly liked farm life, flourished as the queen of her own home. She found our little suburban town with its proximity to the big city a perfect fit. Unfortunately for me she was in too much of a hurry to "help me fit in." The new school clothes she bought me touted to be "the latest thing" and "just what all the other kids are wearing" made me stand out more than fit in. Contrary to her declarations, none of the other kids were wearing purple cords and pink shirts with argyle sweater vests. The jeers and catcalls I got when I showed up in the schoolyard in what she called "the latest Sam Snead look" proved she was completely out of touch and I was paying the price. Sam Snead may have looked great on the golf course in knickers and knee-high stockings but it only gave Gordy Masters an excuse to hang me by my suspenders in the cloakroom. I was used to taking leftover chicken or a pork chop or cold baked beans on cold toast to school as my lunch but she now insisted that I take "a proper lunch" which included salad and fruit and something called Spam between two pieces of Wonder Bread. I tried to trade these delicacies with someone but apparently nobody was into "a proper lunch" but my mother.

The decision that finally sealed my image as a complete doofus, however, came one fateful night at dinner. My mother announced she had enrolled me in Miss Herbert's School of Ballroom Dance for Young Ladies and Gentlemen. I knew about Miss Herbert's dance studio because it was directly above the Malt Shoppe and, more importantly, because it was often a prime target for jokes about "pansies in tutus" and "Herbert's Prance Studio." Once Gretchen and her brother Chrome Dome snuck up to the studio before it opened and spread bacon grease in the middle of the dance floor. Everyone in the Malt Shoppe waited quietly until class started and then broke into uncontrolled laugher and hooted at the top of their lungs as they listened to the young Fred Astaires and Ginger Rogers hit the floor and slide into the walls with screams and groans and shrieks as the grease did its work.   Nobody was seriously hurt, but Gretchen and her brother were found out by Miss Herbert and had to clean up the bacon grease which, according to Chrome Dome was, "The worst shit ever to get off a wood floor!"

My mother tried to convince me that this was "something every young boy needed to learn and that absolutely every kid in town would be doing it with me." I wanted to tell her that absolutely every kid in town would not be doing it and that, if fact, absolutely every kid in town would rather have Doc Seddlemeyer pull absolutely every tooth in his mouth before stepping one foot in Miss Herbert's dance studio. But I knew it would do no good and that it would simply strengthen her resolve that I would go and that I would make her proud. I also wanted to mention that I already had the best dance lesson possible from my great aunt but that would only have helped to seal my fate.

"Jim, tell The Boy what a wonderful idea this is."

My father became deeply engrossed in his meatloaf and uttered something that might have been agreement or disagreement and finally said, "It will probably be good for you, Jackie. My mother insisted I take fencing lessons and fencing is a lot like dancing."

"Dad, fencing is like the Three Musketeers and is very cool. Dancing is for girls and sissies and not cool at all. Fencing is....manly. Can I take fencing lessons instead?"

I had really hoped that my father would come to my defense but he was full blown into his meatloaf now and simply said, "Do what your mother says now. You'll have fun. You might meet a nice girl. Think of that."

He actually had my attention there because I had heard that Mary Jo Halverson took lessons from Miss Herbert and the possibilities began to dawn on me. I remembered holding my aunt so lightly in my arms and moving around the room to the music and it was surprisingly easy to put Mary Jo in my arms instead. This image is what sent me off that next Friday night to the studio above the Malt Shoppe.

My mother insisted on driving me to the studio on the pretext that she had to go uptown anyway but I knew it was more that she wanted to make sure I didn't have an escape plan in mind. A plan that would lead me away from Miss Herbert and toward manly freedom. The plan had certainly been laid and in that fantasy I went in the front door of the studio, up the single flight of stairs and out the window that led to the fire escape that led to the alley that led to freedom. There were several problems with the plan. The first little glitch was that the window at the top of the stairs did not actually lead to a fire escape. To access the fire escape I would have to leap five or six feet to the left, catch hold of the railing and swing onto the steps leading down. A manly stunt to be sure but there was the drop to the paved alley below if I failed. The second flaw in the fantasy was that the fire escape was really accessed from the window in the studio and any number of would-be dance stars, as well as Miss Herbert, would most likely see the flying baby blue pants and pink shirt fall to his death below and report the incident to his mother who, unbeknownst to me, was parked at the end of the alley having anticipated just such a fantasy being played out. The third flaw was the most compelling. I would miss my opportunity to hold the magnificent Mary Jo in my arms. Who knew? Perhaps we would go on to become the next great dance duo, move to Hollywood and who could call me a pansy then? No one! Right? So, narrowly escaping a kiss from my mother I stepped out of the car and waved goodbye.

My back against the brick wall, I carefully surveyed the scene. The park across the street was dark and, at the moment, empty except for the silent Milton T. Whistle standing on his pedestal. To my left Mr. Chambers had just locked up his shop and was headed the other way for what everyone in town knew was a rendezvous with Gloria Spankle. Gloria was Mr. Chambers' most recent conquest which was really no great feat since she had been the object of multiple conquests. According to Gordy Masters, she had even succumbed to his youthful charms. He claimed he had to dump her because as he put it, "She is way too old, man. I mean, I've got my reputation to think of, ya know. I hated to do it and I hated watchin' her cry but I had ta." Nobody believed Gordy. Nobody ever believed Gordy. But Mr. Chambers' affair with the infamous Gloria was a fact. I spent more time looking to my right and the doorway of the Malt Shoppe. To be seen by one of the gang going into 'The Prance Studio' could never be lived down and so, under the cover of semi-darkness and with the speed of a super hero, I made it to the door and up the stairs to the arms of Mary Jo Halverson.

Down below in the Malt Shoppe, the usual gang minus myself, were settling in for their usual Friday night of french fries, malts, Coca-Cola and finding fault with every one and every thing more popular than they. And on the second floor I listened to the music and what sounded like happy voices coming from the behind the studio door. I took a deep breath, straightened my polka dot bowtie and entered. The happy voices went silent and all heads turned to look at me. It was kind of dark and I could make out only a few familiar faces. Some were from my school but most were from Wilson Elementary or the local high school and they were strangers to me. Miss Herbert stepped away from the record player and swept to the middle of the room one hand holding her skirt out to the side and the other extended above her head in a gesture that reminded me of Loretta Young's entrance on her television show. Miss Herbert was not tall nor was she big but she managed to fill the entire center of the dance floor with her presence. She wore her black hair in a severe bun on the top of her head revealing the most striking face I had ever encountered. She had, I supposed, what would be called classic features, high cheekbones, perfectly shaped full lips painted bright red just like in the magazines and dark eyebrows that framed the most beautiful eyes that had ever looked out upon the world. She wore a yellow dress that was belted at the waist and flared out to just below the knee. There was a little chain around her neck and I found it impossible not to let my eyes travel to her throat and then downward to her spectacular....what? Words failed me and I was instantly in love.

"Some of you may know our handsome new student," she began. But I wasn't really listening. I was watching her twist in the half light of the room her arm up and waving like a princess on a parade float including everyone in the room as she spoke.

"This is Jack Laney and he will be joining our little ballroom class starting this very evening"

What was this? Jack? This was a very, very good beginning. I was in love and I was "Jack". Not Jackie. Not The boy. Not Johnny. Jack. A very manly name. Now if I could latch on to Mary Jo this might just turn out to be one of my mother's less destructive plans for helping me to "fit in." The whole idea of ballroom dancing, however, had not really hit me yet. I was so worried about losing the few friends I had found since the move away from the farm or, at the very least, having to endure the humiliation of their jokes and laughter at my expense, that I had failed to realize what was actually in store for me. For the moment I was so dazzled by Miss Herbert and her um...neckline and the fantasies about Mary Jo that the whole picture had yet to come into focus. My burgeoning pubescent hormones were pinballing through my body and both reality and common sense had been left at home in a bottom drawer. Tonight there was only Miss Herbert, Mary Jo Halverson, flashing light reflected off of a mirror ball and... Gladys Cooper? No, no, not Gladys I thought.   Why was Gladys always popping up when Mary Jo was on the horizon. Damn, I thought! I looked frantically around for Mary Jo but much of the room was in shadows and I didn't see her. I was just about to circle the room when Miss Herbert turned off the music and stepped to the middle of the room.

"Now, little ladies and gentlemen, we must begin. Some of you have taken our ballroom class before."

I soon discovered that she never used the first person singular but always said "we" and "our" as though there might be two of her or someone else behind the scenes. Whatever she said was just fine with me. She had a beautiful, kind of throaty voice and I was hanging on her every word.

"And some of you are new to our little group so to start with we are going to pair the newcomers with the more advanced students so that everyone learns together. Are we all fine with that?" And without waiting for a response that might contradict her authority she went on, "Good. Then let us begin."

The pairings started and I listened for my name as I continued to look for Mary Jo. I became more and more panicked as the pairs joined up and the number of us left alone grew smaller and smaller until there was just me, Gladys Cooper, a very tall girl standing like a flamingo against the opposite wall, a couple of boys I didn't know who looked almost as lost as I felt and Roberta Debarras from my school. No Mary Jo. How could this be? Gladys was looking over at me her eyes looking huge through the lenses of her wing-tipped glasses and little beads of sweat began to break out on my forehead. This was going to be a disaster. I was going to be paired with Gladys Cooper.

"Joseph, would you please take Roberta's hand and join the others and.."

I thought I was I going to pee my pants right there. Not only a sissy taking dance lessons but a big doofus who soaked his new baby blue cords right in front of everyone.

"We are going to have Gladys help Peter for the first few dances. Would the two of you please step over with the rest of the pairs? So that leaves Jack and Helen Bird to finish off our lovely couples."

"Helen?   Helen who?"   The girl who walked toward me was a stepstool taller than me. The drops of sweat grew to rivulets. I wasn't sure if it was fear or panic or outright horror that froze me in place.

"Jack, please take Helen's hand and join us. Helen you are our most accomplished student and we are depending on you and the rest of our more experienced dancers to be patient and courteous teachers."

It seemed like it took Helen only two steps to cross the full length of the ballroom and place her hand in mine. It was like putting on a baseball mitt. I now looked longingly at Gladys Cooper.   At least I knew her and she had been nice to me after my encounter with Butch Keller. Anything would be better than the giant who was now escorting, well all right, dragging me across the room.   I glanced over at Gladys with pleading in my eyes. She smiled sweetly and...was that a wink? Did she actually wink at me? It seemed that I was doomed to be humiliated no matter what I did and to top it all off there was no Mary Jo. At least, I thought, I had Miss Herbert and her beautiful neckline to save what was left of a disastrous night.

"Everybody. Please take your partner's hand and find your place on the dance floor. Be sure to leave enough room between couples because we are going to begin with the Cha Cha. Nothing like a good Latin dance to get us warmed up and in the mood for dancing, right class? Cha Cha Cha!"

I didn't feel the excitement that Miss Herbert exuded. In fact, I kept eyeing the door thinking I might make a break for it and be gone before anyone could sound the alarm. I was having trouble seeing around or over my partner who seemed to sense I might bolt because no matter which way I turned she countered to block any dash I might make toward freedom.

Before I could formulate a plan Miss Herbert stepped to the middle of the room and clapped her hands for attention.

"Now pay attention please and we will review the basic steps for the Cha Cha. Now remember, class, the Cha Cha is just a variation of the Mambo and, while the basic steps are simple, the real beauty and fun comes from what we add to it. Think of the rhythm as da da cha cha cha."

At this point she began to demonstrate. She moved very slowly at first forward and back, forward and back. I didn't notice if anyone else was as entranced as I was. I just knew I didn't dare breathe for fear she would stop.

"Listen to the rhythm, class. Listen to the cowbells and the conga they set the rhythm for you. We just relax and let our hips move to the beat"

I watched as she moved, her hips now swaying and swiveling, each few steps taking her in a new direction.

"Couples ready." At Miss Herbert's command each couple took up their position in preparation for the dance. I had no idea what to do and, because escape seemed impossible, I looked frantically around at the others trying to get a sense of what came next.

"Close your mouth and stop gawking at Miss Herbert, Jack, and don't be nervous. Just follow my lead, do what I say when I say and you will do just fine. I am the best dancer here and you will not make me look bad. Do you understand, Jack? Just follow my lead and do what I say. Got it?"

Out of this oversized body thundered a deep baritone voice that, even though she spoke softly, vibrated down my body and into the floor. I was so mesmerized that I hardly noticed she had placed my right hand at the small, if anything on this girl could be called small, of her back and took my left hand in hers. To look into her eyes I would have to have been on a stepladder so I just looked straight forward at her chest and waited for her to instruct me.

"Hold me close, but not too close, just close enough that we can move as one person and when the music starts count with me. One, two, cha cha cha. Got it? Slow, slow, quick quick quick. That's all there is to it. One, two, cha cha cha."

The other couples were starting to practice their

steps so I started to move. I say started to move because the tree trunk in my arms proved immovable.

"Did I say when the music starts? I thought I said when the music starts," she barked.

"Right, ah, Helen. Sorry."

"Follow my lead and do as I say when I say. Got it?"

There was that vibration again quaking through my body. What I didn't know then was that while the young people in 1954 and 1955 were listening and dancing to Bill Haley and His Comets and emerging rock 'n roll, adults (and a handful of geeky kids above the Malt Shoppe) were ballroom dancing to the Cuban rhythms of the Mambo and the Cha Cha. So while my friends were holding each other close as Eddie Fisher crooned "I Need You Now" and The Four Aces harmonized to "Stranger In Paradise" or bebopped around the dance floor to Bill Haley's "Rock Around the Clock," I held Helen "The Amazon" Bird in what is called, in ballroom parlance, the hold position. I stared directly ahead and tried not to focus on her boobs which, I noticed in passing, were barely pushing against her pink fluffy sweater.

Miss Herbert placed the needle on the record and the sounds of Perez Prado filled the ballroom and apparently the very soul of Helen "The Amazon" Bird because at the very first beat she began to count and, much to my surprise, move us both back and forth, back and forth in the hold position. She counted as we moved and just as I thought I might be getting it, she commanded, "when I say 'now' drop your right hand and swing out." I had barely grasped what she said when I heard "Now" so I dropped my left hand and swung out to the left just as she swung out to the right. Without missing a beat she pulled me back to hold and hissed at me,

"The right hand. I said drop the right hand. Do as I say when I say, got it? Try again. Now."

This time I got it right and we swung apart and then moved forward with the same count and then backward and then in hold and out again and, holy cripes, I was doing the cha cha! Just as I had that realization, however, one foot somehow got tangled up with another foot, which may or may not have been mine, and I tumbled onto my back pulling Helen down with me in a jumble of arms and legs ending with me on the bottom smothered in what felt like a thousand pounds of fluffy pink sweater. I couldn't breathe. I was going to die under Helen "The Amazon" and never marry Miss Herbert or touch Mary Jo Halverson's chihuahuas. The harder I tried to extricate myself out from under the mound of fluff, the harder Helen pushed me down screaming at me to let her go.

"Get off of me you little squirt! You miserable little bug! You can't dance! You can't even walk right. You...you..."

Then I saw her. Miss Herbert reaching for me. Her beautiful eyes were filled with concern. Her voice came through the cloud of fluffy pink and landed softly on my ears.

"Oh, my, my, my, are we all right? Are we hurt? Are you hurt, Helen?"

Are <u>you</u> hurt Helen? I was sure she meant to say Jack but then she was lifting the creature off of me and enfolding her in those lovely bare arms while I lay crushed and broken on the ballroom floor. The laughter filling the room above me didn't bother me as much as the sight of Helen and Miss Herbert moving toward the chairs along the wall leaving me on the floor. When I turned away from the image of the two of them ignoring my pain I looked straight into the eyes of….no, not Gladys! Not again!

"Oh, da poor baby. Da poor baby fall down and go boom."

"So, you won't be calling an ambulance or tending my wounds or letting me walk you home?" Gladys had a history of rescuing me after I'd made a fool of myself.

"You better go apologize to Helen right now, Jackie, or you are going to have some real wounds."

"But I tripped. It wasn't…"

"I mean it. Go apologize."

I pulled myself and my pride off the floor and headed toward Helen and Miss Herbert. I may have been limping just a little bit hoping for some sympathy, but they both just glared at me as I approached. I looked at Helen and worked up a real sincere tone in my voice even though I didn't trip on purpose. I might have been just a tiny bit too cocky but, still, it wasn't totally my fault. I mean, she did have really big feet and..

"Don't even think about saying you're sorry, Jack Laney. You are the worst partner I have ever had. How many feet do you have anyway? Four? Six? And I can tell you they are all, all of them left feet. Oh, I hate you Jack!"

She had worked herself into a really agitated state. Miss Herbert kept patting her hand and trying to calm her down. But Helen wouldn't stop and then came the real reason she was so upset.

"Anyway we all know who you <u>really</u> wanted to dance with, don't we?"

Oh, oh, she knew I had been ogling Miss Herbert and that I was, I guess, showing off to impress her. She was going to give it away and embarrass me even more. But Miss Herbert saw Gladys standing behind me and found a different reason for Helen's distress.

"Well, fine then Mr. Laney. Why don't we have Gladys try to corral your many feet for the next dance since our favorite Cha Cha has come to such a sad ending. Gladys, please take Mr. Laney's hand and return to the dance floor. Helen, I am sure Peter would love the benefit of your skills as the best dancer in the room."

Thus she not only put me in my place which, unfortunately, was in the arms of Gladys Cooper, but she had also fed Helen's ego and calmed the moment back to a semblance of order. You had to love her! Gladys took my hand and pulled me away.

"She is not only three times your age, Jackie, she is also in love with Mr. Hunt from the high school and she can actually dance where as you..."

"You mean Miss Herbert? Wha'do I care who she's in love with. You don't think..."

"Come on, Jackie, everyone saw how you looked at her. How you looked over at her with that silly little, 'Oh, look at me, Miss Herbert, see what a great cha cha I'm doing' grin on your face before you tripped

Helen and landed you both on the floor."

"You don't think she noticed do you?"

Before Gladys could answer, Miss Herbert was introducing the next dance to be learned.

""Now class we can't let a little spill spoil our evening can we? Why don't we take a little break and work on a slower but no less challenging dance. In our next lesson we will attempt the Waltz. Considered by many to be the most beautiful and magical of all the ballroom dances. At its best it sweeps us around the room with graceful dips and turns and steps as light as air. Are we ready class? Let us begin by having Helen and Peter show us the proper way to begin our waltz."

Helen and Peter stepped to the center of the floor while Helen continued to give me looks intended to drive knives into my heart. The rest of us took up places to watch and learn. As Patty Page began Tennessee Waltz, Miss Herbert counted one-two-three, one-two-three, putting the emphasis on the first count, and Helen and Peter began moving across the floor. I had to admit that Helen looked almost beautiful as she tilted her head back and just a little to the side. Peter was trying hard to keep up but it was his first try. Everyone held their breath hoping he wouldn't fall. Most of us didn't notice that Helen was lifting poor Peter almost completely off the floor so that his feet barely touched the ground as she moved them both around the ballroom.

"Listen to the music, Peter. Let yourself fall into the music, dear. Very nice. Now everyone let the experienced partner show you how to begin and then join Helen and Peter."

As Gladys turned to face me she glared at me, her eyes huge and angry behind the thick lenses of her glasses. This was not the angel of mercy who had rescued me after Butch Keller slugged me, who had almost let me kiss her on her front porch.

"If you make me look foolish or mess up with your bug eyes looking at Miss Herbert, so help me, Jackie, I will no longer be able to be your friend. Stop dreaming of your future with a woman three times your age and dance with me. OK?"

"OK, OK, I get it," I said.

I placed my right hand at the center of her back the way my great aunt had taught me, took her left hand in mine and began to count in my head one-two-three, one-two- three. It was awkward to say the least but we were moving and not tripping over each other and that was a plus.

"Don't look at your feet, Jackie. Look at me and feel the music move us."

I remembered how light my aunt had felt in my arms and how gracefully she moved to the music in her head. I forgot about Gladys and Helen and even Miss Herbert. I was back in the parlor with my great aunt in my arms. The light reflected across the floor and up the walls and the music took the place of everyone and everything around me so that even as it ended I was still dancing with my aunt and then with Gladys. I didn't feel like a little squirt or a miserable little bug. I felt...wow...

"We can stop now Jackie," Gladys whispered. "The music has ended we can stop." I was suddenly aware of the silence. Everyone was looking at us.

As Gladys and I walked home, I knew I had made a fool of myself with the whole Miss Herbert thing and I knew I wasn't a great dancer but I thought I might go back again to the studio above the Malt Shoppe. What seemed more important, though, was I hadn't lost a friend. Gladys was still my friend. She stepped out in front of me and did a little twirl as she smiled into the stars and the farm loosened its grip a little bit more.

EPILOGUE

Every branch blossoms according to
the root from which it sprung

I pounded the dust out of the leather that was petrified with age and leaned the old mitt against the pillar at the end of the porch.   A cigarette placed between the index and middle fingers and an old moonshine bottle from Perley Kin's still leaning into the overstuffed little finger made an interesting still life, I thought.   Not politically correct today but there was a time when people hadn't been such purists, a time of rare beef and thick, rich cream, and greasy eggs, and good cigars, and booze without blenders. But that time had passed.   In some cases it was buried six feet deep; in others it was covered in layers of dust and rust and weeds that fed on neglect.   The time of the farm had passed.   My time on the farm had passed as well.   I had a very difficult time letting it go, though eventually, I had.

The little lab puppy was sprawled in the shade, content for the moment.   He had spent most of the afternoon with me darting from one sensory point of interest to another like a pinball gone wild. I preferred to take it slowly.   I had walked with care through the old house finding it difficult to imagine I was in the right place.   Some of it was still there.   The pump still clung to the edge of the kitchen sink, not worth the scavenger's effort to remove it.   Part of a chair, a cinder bucket, the shell of Uncle Shay's radio, a few pieces of faded wallpaper were all visible signs of the past. In the parlor, only one iron bedstead was left. Someone had removed or broken one leg so that it remained crippled at the back of the room, too weary to be bothered about the cobwebs or the rain that dripped from the crumbling roof. But only when I closed my eyes did the real smells and sounds come back to me. Only when I ran my hand across what must have been the broken parts of Aunt Jane's bed, could I feel the presence of that other time.

I had walked past the well and out across the fields to Lake Cullen. The little pup bounded in and out of my afternoon and kept me from getting lost. I had sat on top of the dilapidated corncrib and stuck my feet up on the fence rails by the pigpen. I had stopped in the milkshed to kick at pieces of unidentified junk. I had one place left to go. I had saved it for the very last and now I wasn't sure I wanted to see it at all.

I started to retrieve the bottle but I liked the picture it made. It suggested the same dichotomy of images that seemed to characterize my afternoon. The walk to the shed seemed to take a long time. I pushed my way through the four-foot-high weeds that covered every inch of the yard, hoping all the time that the mean-tempered gander that harassed me in my youth was not still out there hissing in the weeds and waiting for its chance.

The shed was covered with vines and, like the rest of the outbuildings, remained standing only by the grace of God. Like a pile of pickup sticks they could all come tumbling down if a single board were moved and the delicate balance upset. The door had been pulled shut and chained. When I finally managed to force it open the sunlight rushed in illuminating the old relic in a flash of dusty gold. She was still there, the old "Johnny Popper." She faced out like a horse in her stable waiting and ready. I didn't want to see the rust and the flattened tires. I closed my eyes and felt along her side 'til I could climb up and sit on the contoured seat and place my hands on the steering wheel. With my eyes closed I could still sense the power. I could still thrill to the magical spell she cast. Something moved inside me, spoke to me somehow of meadows and lakes and hills.

"She'll plow all day and all night and do it day in and day out for just about as long as you can imagine, Johnny," I heard my Uncle Shay's voice echo in the empty rafters.

Finally I opened my eyes. She was sad to look at. The green paint was rusted away and spiders lived in the remains of her cast iron block. Yet, she managed to look like she was ready to put in a full day's work if someone would only dust her off and pour a few drops of oil here and there. I thought about digging out a few tools and taking some time to get her running again. The lab sat patiently by my side waiting.

~ ~ ~ ~

When I looked up, the top of her head had just appeared as she made her way up the hill. Gradually all of her appeared, her hands stuck in the back pockets of her jeans and her shoes kicking up swirls of dust in the sunlight.   Her brother Richard had eventually taken over their farm but his heart wasn't in it and now it was up for sale. She had been down the road doing much the same as I was, collecting memories.

When she got to the shed door she stopped and looked up at me.

"You look like a little kid up there"

"I know, and you look just like a young girl who came walking up to me when I sat on the seat of another tractor long ago."

"You remember her do you?"

"I do. I certainly do. I married her."

"Lucky you", she said

"Lucky me", I said

ACKNOWLEDGEMENTS

The problem with thank yous, of course, is that there is always the danger of inadvertently leaving someone out. So let me say from the beginning that I am very grateful for all of the support and love that has surrounded me over the years and allowed me to follow my dreams. None of us can take full credit for what we achieve. It is only the result of what others have given to us along the way. In particular, however, I must thank Andrew and Patricia Brown, the first of my friends to watch this story unfold and serve as the first of my editors. Also, my good friend Paul Swift, a professional editor, who spent countless hours on every page of this novel and saved me much time and humiliation. I also need to especially thank Frankie White my colleague, friend and remarkable artist who created the original cover design for this book. Finally, my wife Donna who gives me love and support every single day, who is my partner, my soulmate, my companion through life and who I love more than life itself.

49462594R00137

Made in the USA
Middletown, DE
17 October 2017